The Choice

Paul Romano

Bamboo Grove Press

*Books for Persevering Through
the Great Change*

The Choice

Copyright © Bamboo Grove Press 2013

Cover Design: Paul Romano

ISBN 978-0-9821624-7-7   Paperback edition
ASIN B00EBC8P4G   Kindle edition

Printed in the United States of America
First Edition

To my beloved dyslexia whisperer who polishes and illuminates the world around her

Table Of Contents

1. Lucy & Adrian 1
2. Youth 4
3. The Meeting 13
4. The Marriage 21
5. Earth's Vibrational Spectrum 25
6. The Birth of a Champion 36
7. The Law of Attraction 40
8. The Viper Pit 47
9. The Law of Intention 52
10. From Neil to Richard 55
11. The Need for Upheavals 60
12. Lucy's Ethyrical Farm 69
13. The Law of Allowance 83
14. Richard's Prison 95
15. Adrian's Repetitive Behaviors 97
16. Initiation 100
17. In the Weeds 106
18. Obelisks and Radiant Hearts 114
19. Planes of Existence 120
20. The Invisible Battle 125
21. Humanity is Being Groomed 135
22. Those Poor Americans 146
23. The Law of Balance 166
24. Reaching Up 171
25. Becoming What They Ought to Be 173
26. Fusion vs. Fission 183
27. Adrian's Pitch 193
28. Lucy's Letter 202
29. The Choice 210

1. Lucy & Adrian

Deep in the heart of the star cluster known by some as the Seven Sisters or the Pleiades, the great mentors or Entrusted Ones who had long provided counsel to the Celestial Fellowship put out a call for a gathering of special souls. Their purpose was to choose those souls who were well suited to incarnating on Earth at this time in her history that was so fraught with danger and opportunity. Their mission would be to assist humanity with redeeming itself so that the brotherhood of human beings could rise in love at last and take its natural place in the benevolent universe of the Divine Hierarchy.

From all over the galaxy willing beings came to the gathering. Among those who were chosen was a bright and pure soul who was well known to the Entrusted Ones. To her was given the special task of opening herself up right in the belly of the beast so that she could bring into Earthly existence a champion who was destined to lead the human beings of the future to an inner promised land. There, within their heart of hearts, human beings would finally find refuge from a hostile and barren world. There they would discover their true nature and thus become ready at last to take the next step in their evolution.

With the blessings of the Entrusted Ones, this daring soul set herself immediately to her task. She began her life in human form in the small town of Mt. Hope, Ohio on the outskirts of an Amish community in the center of the heart of America. Born during the peace of the early morning hours in the middle of May, she was named Lucy. Her mother realized that this was her name when she witnessed the room filling with light at the moment of her daughter's birth. Lucy was born as strong as she needed to be and as eager to embark on her assignment as was necessary. Her mission was to help humanity remember.

Meanwhile in another part of the galaxy, an ancient and meticulously executed plan was about to come to fruition. On a large and depleted planet that was making an extremely elliptical orbit around a diminishing star, the Great Usurpers still made their home for as long as it was going to be able to hold out. For centuries, the heartless and technologically advanced race of the Great Usurpers had had dark designs on the inhabitants of planet Earth and its resources. For centuries, they had ravenously extracted the Earth's minerals and spirited them away back to their own planet. For centuries, they had compulsively studied her people.

The people of Earth were in many ways an anomaly in this universe, an experiment with tendencies towards chaotic and dramatic swings between evolution and devolution. After a close study of the unique qualities of earthbound humans, the Great Usurpers believed that they had found a design flaw in them which they could exploit and use to unseat the divine essence that had created the universe. The Great Usurpers painstakingly worked to create and execute a demonic plan to separate the people of Earth from the divinity that resides within them so that they could use this energy themselves to overturn all that is. Once the original architecture of the universe was destroyed, the Great Usurpers would use this supreme creative force of harvested soul energy to remake creation. The new universe would resemble the Great Usurpers in every way and they would have complete authority over it. This was their primary ambition as a species.

Among the many of their soldiers who were ordered to incarnate on the Earth for this purpose was a high ranking official who was given the task of creating a tyrant who would drive humanity to its ruin. Born on a frigid day in January into a wealthy and established family in New York City, this soldier was named Adrian by his father as it was a dark day when birth complications took Adrian's mother from planet Earth in a sea of blood and pain. Adrian quickly grew into a restless and driven person who ambitiously embarked upon his assignment as soon as he was able. His orders were to put the finishing touches on the system the Great Usurpers had ritualistically and elaborately constructed over many, many years that had been designed to force humanity to forget.

Thus the stage was set and a whole universe was watching as Lucy and Adrian met, married, conceived a son and did battle each in their own way, thus deciding the future of the Earth.

2. Youth

Lucy grew up into a human more or less like other humans as she had no conscious recollection of her original home. She did have a number of experiences during her childhood that gave her brief glimpses into her real nature, however. Her first memorable experience occurred when she was seven. One night she was lying on the grass gazing up at the stars. Gradually, one set of stars seemed to pull her towards them. As she looked at them, her heart filled with an overwhelming sense of longing. It was a feeling that there was something missing and that what was missing could be found in those stars. This feeling lingered in Lucy for a long time.

Another experience took place when she was twelve. While wandering home from school one day, Lucy found herself in a park near her home. She sat down on the grass in an out of the way spot and idly ate an apple that she had in her backpack. As she relaxed and looked around, the park inexplicably morphed right before her eyes into a different world. Lucy found herself transported to another dimension far away from present day Earth.

Her first awareness of this other place was of its condition. She realized that she was clearly somewhere else because the new place was so light and peaceful. As the vision continued to unfold in front of her, a village of simple buildings constructed out of natural materials became visible as did people who were joyfully moving in and out of them in the course of their daily activities. The sounds of the village blended together in harmonic unison and everything was beautiful and purposeful. In the center of the village, Lucy saw a large open building where many people were sitting in silence. The air was so still and pure around that building that just the sound of her foot involuntarily sliding a bit across the grass she was sitting on seemed harsh in comparison.

Lucy did not know where she was or how she got there

but she did not want to leave wherever it was. She was plunging deeper and deeper into her vision when a stray Frisbee crashed into a bush near where she was sitting. This snapped Lucy back into her earthly reality with such force that she felt as if she had been struck. Stunned, she sat motionless for some time. As she gradually shook off her confusion, she realized that she could still feel the condition of the mysterious place as the remnants of her vision briefly lingered on the air before being pulled back to a higher plane of existence.

This vivid experience heightened Lucy's awareness of the burdensome weight that humans live with on present day Earth. For the next few days, she felt like she was trudging through mud. Everything felt dense and unbearably heavy. She felt like even the air around her was constricting. It was hard to move. It was hard to breathe. It was even hard to think as it felt as if her very thoughts were being confined. Mercifully, after some time, her consciousness of the weight faded and she was able to more or less resume her life as it had been before her vision. She was never again quite the same Lucy, however.

Lucy's experience in the park opened a door for her, ever so slightly, onto the spiritual plane of existence. It provided a kind of starting point. It gave her a small awakening. From then on she continued to have other-worldly dreams and visions from time to time. She also had brief experiences of leaving her body and floating in unknown realms and dimensions. This happened most often when she was under stress. After a little while, she always returned to her body refreshed and invigorated.

One particular experience that repeated itself over and over again through her younger years involved her feeling like an inflating balloon. Often when she was bored in school or was distractedly watching some nonsense on TV, she would have the sensation of expanding. She would grow larger and larger, quickly growing out of her body, and opening out beyond herself. She felt as if she might go on expanding forever. However typically something jerked her back, just as the Frisbee had done in the park, and this would snap her out of her expansion and bring her crashing back to her earthly form. She didn't particularly understand these experiences but she didn't mind them either.

Mostly, though, there were the voices. Lucy heard them throughout her childhood. At first she thought the voices came from her stuffed animals and other toys. But as she grew older, she realized that there was more to them than that. It eventually dawned on her that the voices coming as faint whispers somehow emanated from within her. They were always loving and thoughtful as they spoke reassuring and encouraging words to her so she was never scared or startled when she heard them. She grew used to hearing these voices and came to count on them in some subtle way.

Whatever Lucy set out to do, the voices were there helping her. They were her not so silent inner companions who guided her when she needed guidance and picked her up when she had fallen. As with her other experiences, Lucy did not share the messages that came to her or even the fact that she received messages. It was not that she was embarrassed about them or had a fear of being labeled or ostracized. Rather it was that she instinctively knew that her experiences were too sacred to discuss outwardly.

Lucy otherwise lived a very typical existence. She excelled at school but not in a noticeable way. She played some sports and had some friends. Mostly, though, she was the light of her family. Everyone who knew her family knew that within the coziness of home, Lucy generated so much joy and love that all of her family members positively basked in it. The heart of many a family friend had been touched by observing this.

As she got older, Lucy discovered that what she liked best was to express herself through plants and art. For years, she kept the family garden and grew prize winning vegetables. Somehow what grew in Lucy's garden was slightly more refined and just a tad sweeter than what grew in the other gardens nearby. Lucy's secret was that she looked lovingly into the heart

6

of her seeds and plants and hummed back to them the tune that came to her as she peered into them. Her songs were nurturing on so many levels that the trees and weeds around her garden began to thrive too, as did the animals and insects that made their homes in the area.

Lucy was also a natural artist and felt most at home when she was creating. In fact, she was blessed with an abundance of creative energy. She had such a vivid imagination and innovative spirit that whatever she envisioned seemed to just spring to life beautifully. Lucy took great care and interest in all her endeavors so that even her most mundane tasks were carried out with an artistic quality about them. With her pure and evolved spirit, Lucy could have become anything that she wanted to in this world. Her abundance of creative ideas and creative energy left her with only one true avenue, though, and that was to be an artist in every sense possible.

When she came of age, Lucy chose to attend a small college where she could study folk arts and permaculture and have the freedom to fully explore her artistic expressions in many fields. After graduating she sold many of her creations to obtain income. She particularly sold her pottery, her baskets and her paintings in good number.

Her art was unique and beautiful but it went generally unnoticed by the powers that be in the art world. Her art, like Lucy herself, was in many ways characterized by invisibility. Lucy herself continued to go pretty much unnoticed even on into her adult life. People tended to just look right through her. There had been times when she was the only student with her hand up back in elementary school and the teacher would not call on her. The teacher knew Lucy was there but just couldn't see her somehow. There were people who had known Lucy for years and years and were very fond of her and yet after some time passed, they just could not remember her. It was as if someone pulled the memory of Lucy out of their consciousness. This turned out to be purposeful. It was in the interest of all of the souls volunteering for Celestial Fellowship missions that they be given a protective shield that allowed them to do their work largely unnoticed. For Lucy that meant that she was the girl who was there but was not there.

Adrian, on the other hand, was always very noticeable. In fact, he demanded people's attention right from the beginning. Like Lucy, Adrian had no conscious recollection of where he was from. However, his orders were woven into his genetic fabric. Furthermore, the Great Usurpers watched his every move to make sure he did not get off track. Their consciousness was stuck to him like bubble gum sticks to hair. Their forceful thoughts permeated his every experience and controlled every aspect of his life. Nothing was left to chance including Adrian's reactions and the experiences that created them.

For the Usurpers' plan to be successful there was no room for error. They could not take a chance that Adrian might slip and embrace his higher nature. For their plan to work effectively, he could not be allowed to develop a conscience, learn to love, or develop any of the higher character qualities that human beings flirt with from time to time. For Adrian there was no choice. He was to be what he was designed to be – nothing more and nothing less.

As a child, Adrian found the Earth a dirty, irritating place. There was too much life and too many undeveloped resources. All the green bothered him as well. As time went on, he developed a slight disgust for his fellow humans. There were just too many of them and most of them were pretty much useless to him. He was much quicker than anyone he met. He understood complex problems easily and did not have the patience to wait around for his peers or even his elders to get to where he was. Much of the time, he was acutely aware that he was surrounded by weak and inferior beings. He was also conscious from a young age that where he was today would always be far behind where he would be tomorrow. This acute awareness only aggravated matters for him.

As Adrian grew older, he got into the habit of putting a pretend self out in front of himself as if he were holding up a puppet. Up to this point, whenever he gave honest and forthright responses people typically looked at him in complete horror. He frequently got into trouble with this honesty of his. Adults and peers alike told him that the things he said were not okay. He, of course, was untouched by their opinions because he knew that they were the ones who were not okay. In fact, he was the one who was how people should be. It was everyone else who was not who they should be. They were the abominations. So he developed this puppet persona he called "just like everyone else." He made a game of using this persona, a game that he relished. He took great pleasure in his ability to weave an illusion so powerful that everyone thought that he was a splendid chap.

He learned how to read people in order to understand what they wanted to hear. He learned how to regurgitate the response they wanted in a way that left the other person feeling like he was giving them a gift. He laughed as he thought secretly to himself about how what they took as a gift from him was really a poisonous barb. He used his abilities to extract personal data and manipulate people and systems in a destructive way. He did so with such tact that very few people suspected that he was the mastermind behind all the misery he left in his wake. If a person ever did start to suspect that Adrian was the one creating the pervasive malevolence, Adrian quickly maneuvered to cover his tracks with such ability that he easily made his accusers look and feel crazy.

After a short time spent in perfecting this game, Adrian went on to develop the skill by which he could warp or bend other people's thought processes. He learned to inject ideas and emotions into the systems of his fellow beings without having to even say a word out loud. It was a talent that would serve him well in the future as he set about following his orders. In fact, this was a Usurper-based ability and it was awakened in him through a significant realization that Adrian had in his youth.

On the first day that he attended school as a small boy, a great deal of hostility surrounded him as Adrian just seemed to bring out the worst in people. This phenomenon went far beyond the reactions Adrian got from what he said or did. It went far beyond that because on an energetic level, Adrian emitted such a hostile vibrational condition that other people instantly reverberated to it with whatever their own similar condition might be. It was a subtle thing for the most part, hardly noticeable to the untrained eye but whether consciously noticed or not, whenever Adrian was around there was automatically more fighting, more selfishness, more anger, more hostility in the environment.

Some of this negative energy was bound to come back at Adrian. During the initial years in school, Adrian was indeed the target of older bullies and aggressive classmates. He was also scolded by teachers at times. After years of tolerating these reactions, Adrian made a significant discovery when he was twelve. He learned that he could point his thought force at a human target or a target group of people and, by using his will force, he could attach the negative energy that surrounded him to that person or group of people. Then he only had to sit back and watch that person's life or the group's continuity unravel.

Over time, Adrian learned to perfect this skill as well as other related tricks and techniques. For instance, he learned to use his voice in such a way that he could take a hold of one person's mind, direct it at another person and then project his dark energy through the person he controlled at the targeted person. In this way, Adrian was able to create conflict and change social dynamics without ever being suspected of any involvement. Needless to say, this was another Usurper-based ability at which he was to become quite masterful.

With these two new tools, Adrian became a powerful boy. He no longer received pushback or reverberations from the negative energy that surrounded him as he had learned how to harness that energy and project it at and through other people. So although conflict, hostility, selfishness and malice continued to surround him, people no longer reflected those conditions back at him. In fact, his new found skills gave him a certain stature, a confidence, and also a strong presence that intimidated but also impressed both his peers and the adults in his life. People sensed that there was something menacing lurking behind his dark eyes so they tended to automatically give him what he wanted and stay clear of his path.

As Adrian grew older, more negative entities or dark energetic beings attached themselves to him in order to feed off of the negative energy that surrounded him and trailed after him. These new entities only added to Adrian's power since whenever he pointed his ill will at someone, they too would attack that person. This added impressively to the energetic assault and damage done to Adrian's victims. Over the years, these dark entities grew in power, as did Adrian himself, which eventually made resisting his will all but impossible. All in all, by the time he was a young adult Adrian had enormous firepower. He played at an altogether different level than the people he was competing with. As a result of this, he grew to have a feeling of invincibility which of course later became a weakness – Adrian's' Achilles heel as it were.

Another aspect of Adrian's internal makeup was that he developed a deeply compulsive personality. Repetitive behaviors and an obsession with particular numerical or numerological ways of doing things started when he was a child. They eventually grew into a whole web of repetitive patterns that he strictly followed year in and year out. He felt that with each repetition of any given pattern, the pattern grew stronger and the matrix of the web of patterns became stickier and more encompassing. He found that each time a pattern was repeated, its momentum grew and the pattern seemed to absorb more matter like a snowball rolling downhill. He did not know why this gave him such pleasure but he knew that it was important and right that he follow these patterns.

Adrian's primary compulsion was a lust for power. He

concluded early on that to get more power he would have to acquire wealth and stature. So at an age younger than other children started having such thoughts, Adrian began making career plans. He meticulously studied the system of wealth and power that ruled the world and then he laid careful plans for skillfully working the system. His academic record was impeccable which enabled him to go to the Ivy League school his father had attended. There he made the right connections and joined the right secret society. Upon graduation, his career proliferated like a cancer as the system of life at the time was specifically designed to richly reward people like Adrian with enormous wealth and power.

3. The Meeting

For centuries, human beings have been living according to the Great Usurpers' model of evolution without any conscious knowledge of the condition of the Great Usurpers' existence that suffuses it. Long ago on their home planet, the Great Usurpers chose to equate technological and scientific superiority with evolutionary development itself. They also chose to believe that the use of force, military or otherwise, was the best and fastest way to achieve any objective. Gradually they managed to impose their approach to life and development upon earthbound humans until it was embraced by humans as if they had originated it themselves.

However, unlike their human protégées, these Usurpers or appropriators from Planet X were acutely aware of the universal laws that bind all of creation together. They were equally acutely aware of the consequences of any blatant disregard of these laws. Since their orientation towards the universe was in direct opposition to these laws, they had long been hunting for loopholes through which to exploit the laws rather than put themselves in the position of simply breaking them and suffering the natural consequences. In other words, the Great Usurpers were looking for ways to scam or game the divine natural order.

The Great Usurpers had always been a consumption-oriented race. In the distant past, their rapacious ways had been so extreme for so long that their way of life had thoroughly depleted their planet's natural resources. It had also created such extreme pollution that their world had become permanently contaminated. Imagine how the Earth might be a thousand years from now if all earthbound humans were to continue following their present way of life for all of that time. That was what the Great Usurpers had done and that is what their planet had become. All along the way, they had ignored the warnings from God within, ignored the results of their own experiments, and ignored the hints from the higher developed beings who benevolently advised them. In spite of everything, the Usurpers had fiercely clung to their consumption-oriented ways until their planet was left wrecked and barren. At that point, they exercised the only option they had left. They turned their attention outward towards the universe at large and dedicated themselves to the task of finding other worlds to devour.

One of their discoveries was a small planet on the outskirts of the universe which they believed was far too obscure and irrelevant for any exploits of theirs to draw attention from the Celestial Fellowship. This planet was rich in many of the key minerals and resources the Usurpers needed. Even better, it was conveniently inhabited here and there by an odd array of fragmented populations left over from past failed civilizations. These populations were quite diverse and included some slave races as well as a warrior class that had been left there long ago by another race not native to Earth. Surely such a mishmash of humans could easily be subjugated and put to work for a higher species so the Great Usurpers set up shop there and methodically went about taking from the Earth everything they wanted from it. This undertaking went so well that the Usurpers eventually invested in building a number of permanent pyramidal structures scattered across the planet's surface. These pyramids, as they came to be simplistically called, were used as power sources as well as visual navigation aids for the Usurpers' frequent returns to Earth.

With experience, the Great Usurpers found increasingly effective ways of coercing the underdeveloped human species into harvesting the Earth's resources for them. Since these species felt no allegiance to each other, they were often able to be cajoled into selling their human brothers into slavery for a few shiny baubles here and there. That made it easy to keep the number of workers high enough. Simple bribery and the occasional threat kept all of the earthbound humans at work hard enough. This easy arrangement lasted for a few thousand years or so until the Usurpers came up against a trait in the earthbound humans which they turned out to share – a propensity for aggression and violence. Apparently the people of the Earth had been learning all too well from their demonic overlords throughout this time. They had gradually realized that they didn't need the Usurpers to run this hostile, profitable system as they were perfectly capable of running it themselves. So they turned the appropriators' own technologies against them and shifted forever the way such business was done on Earth.

Even with their technological and intellectual superiority, the Great Usurpers were ill matched against the warlike inhabitants of Earth once they were thoroughly aroused. Furthermore, the unrefined atmosphere on Earth was very challenging for the Usurper constitution. The Usurpers needed a full array of respiratory devices and other equipment just to visit or live there. This put them at a significant disadvantage. Running out of supplies, finding themselves outmanned in the earthbound humans' relentless campaign against them, and having to constantly compensate for the atmospheric liabilities eventually wore the Great Usurpers down. They packed up and left the Earth, soundly defeated.

They did not accept their defeat graciously, needless to say. They set themselves to studying all aspects of these humans very carefully so that they could avenge their humiliating thrashing at the hands of a race they felt was their inferior in every way. It was during this time that the Usurpers made their most important discovery. They discovered that human beings were actually the product of a genetic experiment carried out by another extraterrestrial race and dumped on Earth centuries and centuries before the Usurpers had discovered the Earth. These humans had been left on Earth bereft of any culture, or history, and without the benefit of the natural, slow evolutionary development that provides so many advantages to other highly evolved creatures. But even though human beings had started out without the critical molding and training that natural forces provide, the earthbound human being still had a Soul and the

Godlike power to create. They were capable of becoming the highest of beings or of being degraded to the lowest form of life.

Humans have the same limitless potential as their more highly evolved brethren throughout the universe but, unlike other elevated life forms, the earthbound human is also capable of sinking to the bottom of the evolutionary scale. Once the Great Usurpers made this discovery, they applied their crafty intellects and superior technology to the task of projecting how this anomaly might best be used to serve their ends. How could this quality of earthbound humans be used to achieve their ultimate goal of usurping God's position?

After extensive scientific exploration, the Usurpers constructed a plan for infiltrating the human beings' hierarchical social order in order to employ highly organized methods for surreptitiously degrading humans over successive generations. They were confident that they could engineer the people of Earth into becoming extremely passive and wholly dependent upon a system of their design which they would create and control especially for the purpose. Once the humans were reduced as far down as they could go, then the Usurpers would be able to strip earthbound humanity of its internal connection to divinity as well as strip it of all other natural abilities and skills. They would bring earthbound humans down to their lowest possible form. With the earthbound humans neutralized and their connection to divinity available to be used by the Great Usurpers for their own ends, the Great Usurpers would be well on their way towards usurping God's position with the enormous amount of special energy that would be at their command.

The Usurpers also theorized that for their plan to be successful, they would need to time specific developments in their plan to coincide with the cyclical reversal of the Earth's magnetic poles. Each planet goes through a long cycle of change and readjustment in which its magnetic poles switch polarities among other things. This process of pole reversal can be interpreted as a cleaning or a resetting cycle for each planet. It is a time when old cycles of all kinds end and new cycles begin. It is also a time when life on the planet can take a giant step forward or a huge leap backwards. In the Earth's case, north became south and south became north every 200,000 years or so.

Soul energy is the purest and most potent creative force in the universe. Splitting the human soul energy away from the earthbound humans would leave a tremendous energy free to be harnessed by the Usurpers for creating their own universal system. However, it would require an input of tremendous energy to create that split or fission. After studying the matter, the Great Usurpers decided to use atomic energy to both split the human beings from their souls as well as expedite the process of the poles reversing on Earth. This would allow them to fulfill their plans more quickly.

Atomic power, as it exists on the Earth today, is demonic in nature and is one of the few forces in existence that can destroy the purity of the soul. Disruption of the soul level of only one being releases a profoundly negative ripple effect felt far and wide. The rapacious mining of the soul energy from an entire planet along with the destruction of the planet itself would have a catastrophic effect felt across the universe regardless of whether or not the Usurpers' ultimate diabolical plans had any real chance of success.

The many races that make up the brotherhood of the Celestial Fellowship have all developed their innate ability to connect to all and everything. To such beings, there are no secrets and nothing is hidden. Therefore, they were well aware of the Usurpers' research and their intended plot for the Earth. In response, the Celestial Fellowship ran a number of projection models of their own about the possible outcomes of the Usurpers' plans.

Since their knowledge and connection to the natural order was deeper and much vaster than that of the Usurpers, the Celestial Fellowship had far more data available to them to plug into their formulas. Although all of their projections indicated that the Usurpers' ultimate plan would not be successful, each projection also indicated that if the Usurpers were successful in their objective of destroying the Earth and its inhabitants then the effects on the interconnected universe would be disastrous. No matter how varied the exact outcomes of the projections, all of them ended in catastrophe for the universe.

With this in mind, the Celestial Fellowship called a meeting with the Great Usurpers. The Entrusted Ones informed the Usurpers that they were aware of their designs on planet Earth and that their plans would not yield the results so craved by them. They also informed the appropriators about all of the possible negative effects these actions would have on the rest of the universe. They reminded them that they themselves would not be exempt from these terrible consequences.

To begin to understand the essence of the Usurpers, you have to think about how it would be on Earth if the worst of the worst of humanity was all that survived here. Imagine for a minute people who cut down huge redwood trees that take thousands of years to grow without the slightest inner resistance. Imagine people who drop bombs and shoot children and laugh and giggle like they are playing a video game while they do it or the predator sex offenders who ruin one innocent life after another without showing the slightest remorse or regret. Imagine bankers who make their immoral looting of astonishing proportions legal as they reduce country after country to paupery. Imagine if these types of people – people without a conscience, without empathy, without love in their hearts or any regard for anybody or anything including themselves – were the only humans left. Then on top of that, imagine thousands of years of additional genetic manipulation, weapons development, psychological experimentation and unabashed gluttony being woven into such people. Imagine that all of the noble qualities humans now possess in some measure like the ability to love or the ability to express compassion, generosity, caring and joy were stripped out of humanity's collective genetic code. Imagine all of this, and you will have just an inkling of what the Great Usurpers were like.

So when the Celestial Fellowship made their case to these appropriators, they were met with hatred, contempt and malice. The advantage to being a hero is that you have greater power, more inner resolve, and longer lasting energy than your villainous opponent. You are also supported by divinity itself whereas your opponent is swimming upstream against the natural order of God's will. However, the difficulty in being a hero lies in the fact that to be a true hero you must follow the rules meticulously whereas the villain has apparently freed himself from all rules, at least in so far as his own moral character and choices are concerned. The hero must be respectful and take the longer, more arduous high road whereas the villain takes liberties and shortcuts at every turn. Since the hero takes the longer road of obeying the natural laws that govern the universe, goodwill and providence gradually mount up behind him supporting him to victory. The villain, on the other hand, starts off quickly by taking shortcuts, exploiting loopholes and forcing his will at every turn. However as the game wears on, the trail of broken rules and waves of negative energy begin to pile up and come back at him, eventually bringing him to his knees in complete defeat.

So this is how it was for the Celestial Fellowship. It was by the long, more arduous high road that they had to approach the Great Usurpers. It was against the rules for them to simply impose their collective will on the Great Usurpers no matter how catastrophic the intentions of those appropriators. The universal law of free will maintains that evolved beings cannot impose their will on others or attempt to control their choices. All life forms are allowed to make choices. The Usurpers knew all of this, of course, and reveled in what they considered the crippling weakness of this governing body of the galactic order. With this being the case, then, the Celestial Fellowship had no choice but to join in the game. They went back and revised their own goals and redeveloped their own strategies for rescuing planet Earth in full compliance with the natural laws that govern the universe. They also increased their attention and intentions towards Earth with the hope that they could accelerate progress on this obscure planet that they had originally projected would only be ready to come into the galactic fold many years in the future. In so doing these Entrusted Ones had full faith, as all true heroes do, that in due course they would be victorious as divine will and order always prevail when the time is right

4. The Marriage

It was an unholy union and none in the universe could deny it but it was a union just the same. How Lucy and Adrian came together is one of the great mysteries that can never be fully understood. There was no past association between them in any life on any planet or any past soul association of any kind. They had no shared beliefs or goals. They were each vibrating on such different frequencies that they should have been pretty much invisible to each other. In fact there was very little evidence to indicate that they weren't invisible to each other. However, they came together anyway, married and conceived a son. Only God's will and their willingness to carry out their work on Earth could make that happen.

As Lucy had grown older, the many voices that talked to her began to appear to her in human form. One spirit appeared to Lucy the most often. He was a refined looking older man with brilliant eyes and a deeply loving manner. He was small in stature but his heart seemed to incorporate the whole universe. When he first began to appear to Lucy, she could only withstand the purity of his vibrational frequency for a short period of time. As the years passed, she evolved and could hardly go a whole day without being in his presence. She called him "father" and he called her his "daughter" because that is how it was and how it would always be.

The first time Lucy saw Adrian, she was struck by the sudden feeling that she was looking at her husband. After observing him for some time in various social settings and chance encounters, she was unable to see in him any negative tendencies that a person of her development would otherwise have easily been able to detect in someone as extreme as Adrian. That is how it is for the pure souls. They are light and, therefore, only see light. At times they may sense darkness but it does not appeal to them so they do not look for it. She perhaps could see that she and Adrian were not alike. At times when she was with him, a faint feeling of darkness like a storm cloud slowly blocking the light emanating from her heart passed before her. The fleeting feeling was nothing she could grab a hold of but it was disturbing nonetheless. Worse still, she could not reconcile this with the nagging feeling that here before her was her husband.

It was then that the spirit of her divine Father began to show his form to her. One day she asked him about Adrian. She told him of what she sensed in Adrian and asked him if he were destined to be her husband anyway. Her spiritual father, whose form was nothing more than a wisp of a holograph, looked at her with moist eyes. He did not speak as he usually did but transmitted his thought directly into Lucy's mind. "If you endure this marriage in all ways, it will please us in all ways." Lucy was so eager to please that she consented in her heart to the marriage immediately without giving it another thought. This done, she adjusted herself, opened her heart to Adrian, and began to draw him to her.

Adrian really wasn't the marrying type. His energy was primarily of the destructive nature. He even created in a destructive way. That is, he would consent to dabble in the creative only if it were to build something that could be used to destroy. As marriage is essentially a creative endeavor, he had no real interest in it. However, he did see in Lucy an opportunity to further his ambitions.

At the time of their meeting Adrian was quickly climbing the ladder of sociopaths and gobbling up as much wealth and power as he could attract to himself along the way. At the top of the ladder he discovered that a great many of the men of power and their wives fancied themselves collectors and appreciators of art. Personally Adrian had no interest in art. In fact he was often repulsed by it but he realized that in order to move in the inner circle, it would be strategic for him to marry someone who could take this bullet for him of appreciating something as ridiculous as art.

In Lucy he saw someone who could fill this need. Adrian

did not relate to people through affection, companionship or relationship. Rather he looked for people to fill roles or perform services that fit into his overall quest for absolute power. He could see that Lucy would do just that. She would fill in the holes of art and culture and social ability that he needed to relate to the women behind the men of power. Also she could provide him with an heir who would continue his life's work when his time was up. But there was more to it than just those two things.

It is a well known fact that opposites attract. The hero and the enemy define each other. The greatness of the enemy dictates how great the hero will become. In a need based universe, you are only given sufficient skills and power to perform the task at hand. Nothing more and nothing less is given. So for both Lucy and Adrian, their union represented an opportunity to play in the big leagues. Their marriage and ensuing conflict would become the fulcrum of an epic war between good and evil that would shake the universe.

So the normal reasons for marriage did not apply here. Both Lucy and Adrian were driven by assignments that vibrated in the very centers of their beings. From birth every cell, every movement and every experience that Lucy and Adrian each had was focused on their respective life goals. It would be hard to describe the level of commitment, attention and drive that animated both Lucy and Adrian. Everything that they each possessed went into the accomplishment of their assigned tasks. There was nothing wasted.

In terms of any kind of love in their marriage – well what can one say about love in such a marriage? One spouse was the embodiment of love while the other was incapable of it. To observe that Lucy did not love Adrian would not be quite correct as she loved all things as a matter of course. It was her nature to love and to be loving. Although there was love in everything that Lucy did for him, she did not really love Adrian as a wife loves her husband.

Adrian, for all of his malevolence, was cultured and polite. He was not violent, crude or vulgar. It would be hard to say that he was respectful of Lucy as he did not respect anything or anyone. However, Lucy's stature demanded a certain level of respectful treatment. When Lucy came to Adrian, she was as pure as the wind-driven snow. Adrian could see that she was a prize and winning that prize appealed to him. He also knew that there was a creative power in her, a power that did not exist in him and that he therefore could not wield himself. He imagined that he could harvest hers, though, and use it for his own destructive purposes so he related to her enough for that.

So that is all that needs to be said about Lucy's and Adrian's wedded life. They were not truly a couple and their marriage was nothing more than a necessary event in this story. Their marriage was not important to either one of them but without it they would not have been able to fulfill their purpose. Without it there would not have been a resolution to the age-old conflict that was about to boil up, overflow and engulf the entire Earth.

5. Earth's Vibrational Spectrum

By the time Adrian began to acquire power and status in his earthly existence, most of the Usurpers' plans for degrading humanity had already been well accomplished. The Great Usurpers had worked through countless incarnations for many generations to recruit untold numbers of earthbound humans to their cause. Through them, the Usurpers had infiltrated the power structure of every country in the world by co-opting human leaders at every level. These human dark planners took their orders from the Usurpers through an array of highly effective networks. Some of them also regularly performed rituals and prayed to their demonic overlords in order to keep the connections open and the power flowing.

The Usurpers used these open channels of communication to transmit their orders to their human cohorts. The dark planners they worked with were a mixed group of Usurper souls incarnated into human form and natural born earthlings who lusted for the knowledge and the power the Usurpers dangled in front of them. This mixed group of servants received and then carried out their assignments in a hypnotized stupor undetectable to other humans.

The web the dark planners wove developed out of periodic, secret meetings in which they made plans to infiltrate organizations of all kinds on local and regional levels, country by country. They used the wealth, power and knowledge given to them by the Great Usurpers to attract local leaders to their secret organizations. Just enough information and no more was filtered down to members on each level of the pyramid of power – enough to enable each group to carry out its specifically assigned work. Only a very few members at the capstone of the pyramid knew the bigger truth and saw the connections. The rest of the members of the organization were given whatever information, truthful or not, that would keep them guiding their local governments along the path set up by the Great Usurpers. That was all that mattered.

In this way, the Great Usurpers exerted an increasingly controlling voice in organizations of all kinds around the globe. They planted their seeds in even the most remote places on Earth in order to ensure that their diabolical plan would sprout everywhere all at once. As these seeds started to germinate in every culture around the world, the Usurpers effectively convinced humanity that the way to happiness was through wealth and power, through technology and force.

A rigid class structure was established and a hazing process put in place all over the world which only permitted those people with intelligence, talent, ambition and skill to rise to the top after they had been co-opted by the dark side. This system grew rapidly and, in due course, the entire earthbound human power structure received its orders from the Great Usurpers in one way or another. The system maintained itself by restricting virtually all earthly wealth and power to a few controlling families that retained global control generation after carefully bred generation. You could not rise to a successful position without the blessing of or, more accurately, the cursing of these ruling families.

Even if you were a good person with good intentions, you still had to bend before the malevolent will of the few dark lords. Kneeling and kissing their royal rings was made more palatable by the stories these so-called elites spun. They were expert at generating excuses and rationalizations for their greedy and hostile plans. In fact, it was their custom to frame their dark plans as a way to "help the masses".

In modern times, their goal of world dominance eventually became casually referred to as "globalization." It was generally considered to be a benign way to connect everyone under a single ruling body for their own good. It naturally followed, however, that onerous taxes were levied to pay for the enormous military force needed to keep the system in line and coercive oppression in all of its forms was imposed to condition the masses to this new world order. The ruling elite believed that they were organizing their coming rule of the world but, in reality, they themselves were being controlled by the Great Usurpers who were planning to destroy all of humanity. With their detailed knowledge of every human weakness, the Usurpers had created endless ways to mercilessly exploit all of them. Their system of wealth, power and addiction swiftly spread across the globe like a plague. The degradation of humanity had commenced full force and was now advancing with increasing speed.

All over the globe, people had been induced into leaving behind their families, their farms and their villages to migrate to the big cities. While working at their repetitive, narrow jobs and living uncomfortably fractured lives, their connection with the natural world and their many land-based, problem-solving skills and abilities developed over generations had gradually begun to dry up and blow away. Their inner connection to the divine had withered as well. Thus had begun the great forgetting process which eventually would bring humanity to its knees. Over hundreds of years, modern day earthbound human beings had become completely dependent upon a system designed and controlled by their enemies. By the time Lucy and Adrian had arrived, they had no primary skills, no knowledge, no inner wealth, no connection to each other, and no wisdom. They had poor character, debilitated health, a short attention span, a growing sense of entitlement, hostile and aggressive personalities and a self-loathing and self-destructive mentality that drove country after country into the ground.

Any hope of humanity regaining all of this lost ground was undermined by the many poisons the dark planners had insinuated into every level of their existence. There were poisons in their water and in their food. There were poisons embedded in the walls of their homes, in their clothes, pillows and blankets. The air was poisoned as well. Electricity, an irritating and aggressive energy, surrounded humanity in every way, crackling and pulsating, attacking the human nervous system right down to the cellular level. An intricate web of radio signals and TV transmissions encircled the globe as well, impeding thought and confusing the masses.

Perhaps the most toxic poison of all was the cultural one. The venomous leaders who were doing the bidding of the Great Usurpers filled humanity's hearts and minds with the most destructive lies and beliefs that they could dream up. By the time the modern computer era was upon them, each human was incessantly bombarded by a host of addictive and hostile stimulations. These stimulations came in the form of television and radio programs. They came in the form of internet media, movies and advertising. They came in the form of vehicles, gadgets, and jewelry. They were found on the streets, in malls, in schools and everywhere else. Each bit of programming, advertising, brain washing was absorbed by the modern day human's system and then silently activated.

These downloaded and then randomly activated programs reshaped the modern day earthbound human into one of the lowest caliber of evolved organic beings to be found throughout the universe. The programs encouraged people to behave in hostile and selfish ways. They made people seek their fulfillment in a world of decadence and illusion. This well-crafted conditioning of earthbound humanity was the most important element of the Great Usurpers' assault. Cleverly, they had designed their Earthly power structure to be held together by the very people they had made completely dependent upon their system. People came to base everything – their self-esteem, their happiness, their success and the very essence of who they were – on this hostile material system that had been designed by their ancient enemies who were working for the total destruction of them and everything that they held dear.

Earthbound humans became rigid and narrow minded. They believed that all there was anywhere was only that which existed within what they saw and experienced in their own small, individual worlds. From this, they began to believe that they were the most superior beings in the universe and that they knew everything or would surely know everything very soon. They felt that they had made it. Their proof was their lifestyle or what they called their "quality of life". They believed that they had reached the pinnacle of what a material being could achieve. They believed that they themselves were the gods of wealth and power. This more than anything else was a pure victory for the Usurpers.

The key to the Usurpers' ongoing success was their coercing the earthbound humans into externalizing God. Domesticated animals present us with an example of the effectiveness of this method. In order to become domesticated, animals must first be stripped of their dependence on nature. This is particularly the case with animals that have abusive masters who demand that they live in a way that violently opposes what is natural to them. Once their dependence on nature is stripped, the unfortunate animals become fully dependent upon their owner and do whatever is asked of them. Only a massive effort to regain their instinctual lifestyle could allow them to break free of their bondage but this rarely happens.

For higher developed beings, the initial step towards enslavement involves disconnecting them from the divinity that resides within them. People who are disconnected from the infinite store of divine love in their hearts suffer deeply in two ways. First, they become depleted as they are being deprived of the greatest nourishment in the universe. Secondly, the nourishing love that also serves as a guiding light that directs an evolved being along their righteous path is no longer felt or even recognized, leaving the person without a goal or directions. Once these two conditions of depletion and disorientation are created, people are forced to look elsewhere for nourishment, guidance and an overall purpose to their lives. They will desperately consume anything to fill the painful void within. They are lost and scared and will accept pretty much anything as guidance, no matter what form it might take. They lose the ability to discern what is real from what is spurious so they do not even detect that they are being starved and misled. They are left without any true purpose for being. They are deeply vulnerable to whoever might be holding the puppet strings.

The Great Usurpers were master puppeteers. They literally wrote the book, our book, on oppressive tactics and systems. They could make people wrongly define love as gifts, promotions, false praise, flat screen TV's, iPhones and pleasures of all sorts. They could make people totally forget about the enormous internal gift of having a soul, a Self, a portion of the creative force that imagined the universe into existence. Once people ignored real love and then later completely forgot about the internal jewel that resided within their hearts, that jewel could easily be plucked away at a moment's notice.

This shift away from inner wealth towards outer so-called wealth was accomplished through the two chief avenues of religion and science. The people of Earth were either persuaded to believe in a God outside of themselves or to not believe in God at all but only in what was called science instead. The people who believed in an external God gave away their power in so doing. While waiting to be rescued by this God of theirs, they lost their ability to connect with the divinity that was waiting inside of them all along. The people who denied God altogether by putting science in God's place believed that nothing existed beyond their material experience. They became hopeless, cynical and hard. Both types of people were trained to look outward for everything. Earthbound humans were now close to being ripe for the plucking.

It was at the beginning of this harvesting time that Adrian embarked on his climb up the pyramid that is the modern day earthly power structure. As soon as he achieved becoming a dominant player in this realm, he and his comrades started receiving instructions on how to put the finishing touches on humanity's great forgetting. They were then charged with collapsing this abomination of a system and bringing the now totally helpless and dependant humanity to its knees.

The modern day earthbound human's world now consisted entirely of elements carefully put into place by the Great Usurpers and their human cohorts. Once Adrian and his crew collapsed this system, the weak and dependant people of Earth would collapse along with it almost immediately. The Great Usurpers projected that once the world as the earthbound humans knew it was obliterated, the humans would quickly break down to groveling before their false, externalized gods with no thought but that of begging to be saved. In this moment of engineered planetary despair and victim consciousness, the Usurpers would be able to swoop in and tear the souls away from these groveling masses. Once they had appropriated this precious energy of infinite potential, the Great Usurpers would use it to become gods themselves.

There was, however, still some hope for humanity hidden away in the very element that the Usurpers hoped to exploit. It is a rare occurrence when opposing sides both need the same major event to occur for the successful completion of their respective tasks. Such was the case in this modern day universal battle, however. For as long as people have been on the Earth, souls from the many different beings that make up the Celestial Fellowship have incarnated on Earth as human beings. These benevolent beings have come to Earth to help move the experiment that is earthbound humanity along the spiritual evolutionary path. These souls take human form for multifaceted reasons. They come because it is their duty and because sometimes it is God's will. They also come because a life as a human being offers unique possibilities for personal spiritual evolution.

It all comes down to vibrations and love. Everything has a vibration. The entire universe is a grand concert with each life form and each object playing a melody that joins together with others in a harmonious convergence or fusion. Love, or God, is the purest form of this melody. Love, or God, has the most subtle vibrational condition. It can be called the vibrationless vi-

31

bration. It is the vibration that can only be detected by the most refined instrument in the universe, the heart of an evolved being.

Love, or God, is the original condition. Everything else in the universe was and is created from this medium. Everything else is a more complex creation arising out of this original condition of God, or Love. The more a creation resembles the original condition of God, or Love, the subtler the vibration of that creation. The farther away a particular creation is from the Creator, the grosser and less refined are its vibrations. One example of such a range of vibrations is sounds. Here on Earth, for instance, we might start with the sounds of nature, move to the beautiful tones of a symphony, and then on to the noises of heavy machinery, the sound of heavy metal music and finally the sound of the screams of a tortured human. On one end we have natural sounds that are the closest to God while on the other end of the spectrum we have loud aggressive noise or wildly painful sounds that are totally out of sync or harmony with the original divine melody.

Each created being has a range of potential vibrations from which it can resonate. Herein lays the greatest attribute and the greatest weakness of the earthbound human being. Of all of the evolved life forms in the universe, the human being has the greatest range of frequency. The human being is capable of resonating on the subtlest vibrational frequency which is only a hair's breadth away from the divine. It is also capable of emitting the most vulgar, out of sync, disharmonious vibrations that have ever scourged the universe. Humans are capable of humming as saints or howling as sinners.

The possible risks and rewards for beings from other places who choose to incarnate on Earth in human form are great. Often, their original planet's vibrational frequencies are so subtle that they only have access to a narrow range of experiences there. All of their experiences are closer to God and the natural order supports them through everything. Yet these refined beings may still have some spiritual issues to work out with anger, depression, fear, abuse and/or victim consciousness. On their home planets, they are limited as to how much such conditions can be experienced and mastered. There is so much love there that the frequency of the undesirable condition never shows up as more than a faint whisper.

When one of these evolved beings incarnates on Earth, however, their latent condition of anger, let us say, can become a roaring inferno of rage with little support around for managing it. In this way the challenges, temptations and pressures that are involved in the polarized life of a human on Earth can create profound opportunities for these higher developed souls to further master themselves, acquire skills and inner knowledge, and make great leaps in their spiritual evolution. Nowhere else in the universe is there such potential for growth as on Earth and in no other time in history is it better than now to grow and evolve here.

However, there is also an enormous risk. There have been many evolved beings who have incarnated on Earth to help humans move along the evolutionary path only to succumb themselves to the dense vibrational condition of this planet. Either through the temptation of a sensory condition or by getting overwhelmed by the moaning masses, higher developed beings have lost their way here at times and devolved to a permanent human status in which they themselves are trapped like everyone else. Then they too have had to reach up into the spiritual stratosphere and go through the long process of liberating themselves from this place of life and death so that they can regain their universal citizenship. This dire possibility actually plays into the divine plan as these trapped higher souls are gradually forming a powerful body of potential warriors who will hopefully tip the scales for the Celestial Fellowship when the time is right.

For the Celestial Fellowship's plan for the upliftment of the Earth to be successful, they needed the current system created by the Great Usurpers to be destroyed. They needed to awaken to full consciousness their potential warriors as well as the native born earthbound humans who have developed their spiritual capacity over the years. Then the Entrusted Ones would be able to work toward helping their earthbound pioneers bring their collective consciousness into harmony with the divine plan. Once this subtle awakening began, many other earthbound humans would also be touched and affected and a grand opening of hearts would undoubtedly take place. When sufficient numbers of the human population were once again ruminating on the divinity in their hearts, a great evolutionary step could be taken and life on Earth would change forever. However, none of this could happen while the system created and controlled by the Great Usurpers still dominated the Earth.

And so it was that both the Celestial Fellowship and the Great Usurpers needed the same kinds of events to take place and were counting on the same gift/flaw in the human being to assure victory for their respective sides. The Great Usurpers had worked to bring the human being down to the lowest possible frequency. From there they believed that they could collapse human psyches and steal their souls. Their projection models told them that human beings were so lowly that once they were brought to darkness, they would forget themselves, embrace the shadow and plunge into the abyss.

The Celestial Fellowship saw things differently. Their projection models gave them a more favorable outcome. Like the Usurpers, the Celestial Fellowship needed the complete collapse of the modern day human civilization. They needed the human being to hit rock bottom as well. However, they believed that if enough people regained and retained their inner connection to the divinity that resides within their hearts, then the collapse of the material world would shock them into remembering and reaching for the light. Once this group created a path to the light, others would be more likely to see it as well and follow in increasing numbers.

The projection models of the Celestial Fellowship told them that materiality on Earth had become so dense and oppressive that the earthbound humans could not evolve until the system that bound them was destroyed. Earthbound humans needed to free themselves of this heavy materialistic abomination. Even though the manipulations of the Great Usurpers had coerced earthbound humanity into living within this system, the humans themselves had also made choices that permitted and maintained it. The Fellowship's projection models clearly indicated that for the people of Earth to fully resonate at the divine level they were capable of, they had to first destroy their addictive material system.

Once their false world collapsed, they would soon breathe a collective sigh of relief and once again begin to hear the faint hum of the divine vibration of love that radiates from within the core of their hearts. They would plunge inward to grab a hold of this precious condition and never let it go again. The many highly developed extra-terrestrial souls trapped on Earth along with the native Earthlings who had achieved some spiritual evolution of their own were already consciously and unconsciously craving to return to the original condition. This broad group had now been activated and called to duty by the Celestial Fellowship. Their craving constituted the hope for humanity and the universal order.

Lucy was among those bright lights who radiated subtle vibrations in the hopes of ennobling the people of Earth. At the same time, Adrian and his group worked to create low frequency vibrations in order to make humanity heavier and heavier. How earthbound humans would respond to these two polarizing vibrational conditions would decide the fate of their world.

6. The Birth of a Champion

The masses slept on contentedly blithely believing in their leaders' lies. Their hypnotized state, so carefully maintained through the internet, media, cell phones, video games and meaningless contests of all sorts, made them painfully unaware of the fact that the Earth and its inhabitants were on the cusp of the greatest epic battle that the planet had ever seen. They steadfastly ignored the many signs and warnings that unprecedented upheavals were in the offing and that these upheavals would surely bring unfathomable destruction and chaos.

The haze that had infiltrated people's brains and disrupted them from firing properly was caused by a soup of electrical poisoning, fluoridated water, pesticides, drugs and vaccines, genetically modified and industrial foods and the total break in their relationship with the nature that was designed to support them. It was literally impossible for them to grasp the vulnerability of their state. Their emotional and egoistic fragility made them create defensive mental walls against the massive overwhelm that was always waiting to assail them. The web of power that controlled them was so densely woven that penetrating it to get to the truth of their lives was all but impossible. Instead these lonely Earthlings remained mentally and spiritually asleep, disconnected from their true potential.

In the depths of this time of awful disconnection, during the quiet of a summer night in early August, a hero was born who was destined to tip the scales of this epic battle either one way or the other. Lucy's and Adrian's only child arrived without much pomp and circumstance but the anticipation and the hopes of both sides in this epic battle rode squarely on his small shoulders.

At the time of the birth Adrian was away on business, as he often was, so Lucy knowingly slipped away from their dark mansion, as she often did. Her instincts led her away to her small farm in the mountains which she had purchased shortly after college and to which she often retreated. A day after her arrival, she started having contractions in the early afternoon. She realized that she felt so comfortable with how the birth would go that she could forgo an unnecessary trip to the hospital. Instead she decided to have a quiet, private delivery with just herself and her beloved baby sharing the blessed event. With these arrangements settled in her mind, Lucy was able to relax into the process and allow the natural guardians who watch over such events guide her through the birth. When her son eventually emerged gently into the world, Lucy scooped him up and held him to her breast. Both mother and child faintly glowed in a way that matched the serene mist that had settled into the valley outside of Lucy's home.

Adrian was not able to see the baby for several days. When he finally did meet his son, he insisted on the name Richard for him as he was hoping he would become a despotic king. Some months earlier while Lucy was carrying the child, she had heard the name Neil for him. She knew then that this was his name as her unborn son was destined to be a champion. She could hardly bear the name "Richard" with which Adrian had swooped in and branded their son. It felt like such a twisted perversion of what the life that had just been inside of her was meant to become. After some internal struggle, though, she conceded the point as the supportive, dutiful wife that she was and settled instead for having Neil as her child's middle name. She never, ever called him Richard as she knew that "Neil" was the true name of her gallant son. She trusted that the unfolding of her son's natural destiny would wash the "Richard" off of him, leaving only the "Neil" behind to fulfill his great spiritual purpose.

With time and her spiritual guide's help, Lucy came to understand that her son's binary name itself represented the core conflict in this epic battle between his two parents and the universal forces they each represented. Already the universe was waiting with anticipation to see whether the boy would become the man "Richard", the despotic and hateful corporate king who would tax the very souls out of his people on the Usurpers' behalf, or "Neil", the noble champion who would lead his people in an inward direction toward their hearts where they would regain the remembrance of their divine inner nature.

In terms of his own placement in this epic battle, Richard (or Neil) was well chosen for his task. He was an old soul, one who was original to this Earthly experiment. His was among the originals that were first unloaded on the Earth hundreds of thousands of years ago. Like everyone else, he had had many lives with varying outcomes. He had had lives in which he had risen to a high spiritual level with all the accompanying good character and loving personality only to experience a spiritual fall before he died. In fact, he had climbed the ladder of spiritual evolution over and over again, in life after life, only to get caught up again and again in repetitive and destructive patterns that inevitably dropped him back down into the abyss before he managed to finish with that life.

He had had a life during which he was a good king who had eventually become corrupt and ruthless. He had had a life in which he was a criminal who had eventually repented. He rose and fell and fell and rose life after life. He got very close to exiting his endless rounds of life on Earth many times only to be pulled back down again and again by the deviant elliptical behaviors that he had created and strengthened in himself through the repetition of many past lives.

In his last life which had ended a relatively short time ago, Richard had become completely overwhelmed by the modern world. He had become so disenchanted with the heavy condition of the current age that he had simply given up. He refused to move forward or backward. He refused to go up or down. He simply shut down his system and waited for his life to end. It ended quickly. At that point the divine forces in charge of such matters yanked him right back into the game without even the slightest time to rest and process his last endeavor on the physical plane. He was placed smack down in the middle of an enormous conflict. In this life, he would finally have to choose once and for all.

Both sides had good reason to be hopeful that he might be either inspired or coerced into joining their respective campaigns. Adrian and his overlords strove to control every element of Richard's life in order to guarantee a successful outcome of their plan. Lucy and her advisors sought in every way to support the inner connection between Neil and the divinity that resided within him. Both sides worked on many planes of existence to bring the young lad into their fold for he was not only destined to choose one path or the other, but his choice would ultimately decide the outcome of this conflict.

7. The Law of Attraction

It is a well known principle that our thoughts, goals and actions attract to us conditions and experiences of similar kind. According to this reflective principle, or the law of attraction, all that we are, think and do is mirrored back to us. What dwells inside of us manifests outwardly in our material lives. In other words, we get back from the world what we give to it. A corollary of this law is that what is inside of us, we see outside of us but call that "the world". While a good and honest person sees the world as a more or less good and honest place that is generally populated with good and honest people, a thief tends to see a world of theft and thieves.

Both the law of attraction and its corollary can better be understood in light of the fact that everything has its own vibrational frequency. With respect to the law of attraction, a being's vibrational frequency resonates out and calls back to it similar vibrational frequencies from the environment much like an echo returns to the original voice. A refined person emits a subtle vibrational frequency so the same sort of refined vibrations often return to them. A person with a lot of anger and hatred in their system emits a grosser vibrational frequency insuring that similar angry and hateful vibrations come back to them.

The corollary that people see outside what they have inside can be explained also through vibrational frequencies. A being's personal vibrational frequency emits a signal much like radar or sonar. This signal automatically reveals similar frequencies or characteristics in the external world to the person sending out the signal. This is why a kind person and a suspicious person can both look at another person and see two rather different people. The kind person sees kindness in the person. The suspicious person sees someone to fear. The reality is that the other person contains both kindness and suspicion. Both qualities are there to be perceived by those who are themselves tuned one way or the other.

40

Furthermore, the vibration a person emits not only reveals already existing similar vibrations "out there" but also creates similar effects in others. For example, if a happy person walks into a room, their happiness is infectious. It radiates out and has a positive effect on others in the room. Similarly if an angry person walks into the same room, the people in it will tend to become angry or fearful in reaction to the aggressive vibrations emanating from that angry person. The happy person causes others to relax their body posture and open up. The angry person causes people to assume a defensive or protective stance. So in many ways the vibrations radiating out from within a person materially affect the outer world, thereby causing the outer world to give similar responses back to that person. That is why we reap what we sow; we attract back what we give out.

This law of attraction was in full effect when Richard Neil was born. Humans working for the Great Usurpers had always been required to possess a substantial level of hatred for humanity. They could not carry out their destructive work unless somewhere inside of them they had a deep loathing for the human race. But being in human form themselves, these workers and dark planners for the Great Usurpers were always riddled with self-loathing as a natural consequence of their positions. Therefore, when Adrian finally looked at his newborn son, he was not able to really see him. He looked and looked away. He was not at all impressed.

Adrian, of course, had the necessary festering hatred for himself and humanity so seeing Richard left him feeling cold. The child had nothing to offer him right now. He was just a human baby who would later grow into a human adult. Adrian saw that he could not shape the baby towards his ends while Richard was still in this early stage of development so he thought to himself, "Let his mother have him for now and when she has made him strong, I will turn him into my heir."

As Adrian had important business matters to attend to and a corporate power structure that urgently needed climbing,

41

keeping his distance from his wife and newborn son suited him just fine for the time being. After having worked his way up the banking ladder at a dizzying speed, Adrian was now fully engaged in making the worldwide connections he needed to carry out the Usurpers' orders. He couldn't jeopardize all that he had accomplished so far by wasting time on his family. Besides, he had become quite uncomfortable around his wife.

For years Lucy had been in the habit of waking up during the peaceful hours in the middle of the night, usually between 2 a.m. and 4 a.m., and meditating. Her meditations and the messages she received during them were of great comfort to her. But the vibrational condition that emanated from her while she drifted into her samadhi was quite unnerving to Adrian. He invariably had very disturbed sleep and restless dreams during those times. When he awoke, he often felt rattled and unsure of himself which were feelings that he detested. So he had purposely done all that he could to keep a great deal of physical distance between himself and Lucy. Now that Richard was born, he planned to put even more miles between them. There was something about the creation of a new human life that unnerved him. So without skipping a beat, Adrian continued to tend to his banking empire. For seven years, he left Lucy alone to raise Richard by herself.

Those seven years turned out to be the sweetest of Lucy's life. In her little Neil, Lucy did not see a potential despot. She did not see a hateful narcissist who could bring humanity to its knees. She saw only the love that she had for him. She felt only the love that he drew from her. A mother's love is such a wonderful thing. Any baby that is placed in a bubble created by the love of its mother for the initial years of its life can become anything in this world. A newborn nurtured by love from the start and all through those primary years grows strong in many ways.

As a matter of fact, one of the Great Usurpers' methods for disempowering humanity took special aim at the very early life of humans with the creation of a system designed to destroy the mother–child bond. Many mammals are not fully developed enough to really be in the world at birth. Earthbound humans are among this group so a newborn baby needs to always be wrapped in an external womb made of its mother's love and care. However in the system designed by the Great Usurpers and their earthbound henchmen, a newborn baby is taken away from its mother the moment it is born and immediately given poisons in the form of so-called medicine. It is poked and prodded and generally given a rough welcome into the world. Male babies even have a traumatic operation done to the most sensitive part of their bodies within days of birth that carries lifelong consequences.

The system in modern times has devolved into taking the baby home from a hospital and then placing it in a small prison cell for much of its time where it may cry desperately to be close to its mother's heart. The baby needs to be in close proximity to its mother for those early years getting nurtured and maintained in all ways by its mother's love. However in this diabolical system, the caged baby is taught to be alone. This lesson is not easily learned. The baby longing for its mother wails for human contact. The baby soon learns that its cries are falling on deaf ears, however, and it simply gives up and begins to harden against the world. The mother and father are often heartbroken by their child's cries but having been brainwashed into this way of life, they believe they are doing what is best for their baby by letting it cry. They are teaching it independence, they are told. However in the mother's heart, she knows that this is not best.

A mother is filled with a divine love that is intended to flow into and surround her vulnerable child. The child needs this love as much as it needs its mother's milk. But within the hostile system put in place to undermine humans by the Great Usurpers, the mother does not give what she must and so the child does not receive what it must. Both suffer. Developmental milestones critical for mother and child both are not reached. This system does not kill the child or the mother outright but enormous damage is done to both of them. This is damage that cannot be fully repaired. Connection and intimacy between the pair is weakened and unless their course is corrected, it will only get weaker as the years pass. As a matter of fact, the damage also increases dramatically over time as this weakness is passed on from one generation to the next. The effects from this hostile system accumulate.

The young child is then shipped out of the home too soon to daycare, preschool and school. The child who spends most of its waking hours away from its family is mostly raised by the system created and controlled by the Great Usurpers' earthly minions. Through this the child is stamped and molded by the earthbound humans' ancient enemy. The purpose of the system is to harden the hearts of each succeeding generation of people, cutting them off from each other and the divinity that resides within them. Once this indoctrination is completed, it is almost impossible for the hardened adult to become what they were originally meant to become.

This was not the lot of Neil, however. The Usurpers cannot yet force a mother to separate from her child. They can only pressure, confuse and entice mothers to make that choice themselves. Lucy knew what was natural and that was to keep Neil close to her for those initial years. She ensured that those first seven years of his life were magical ones. Lucy taught Neil all that she knew. The two lived out on her mountain farm and explored the natural world together. Early on, Neil was fascinated by wildlife and explored all the nooks and crannies of the garden and woods in the natural setting he was so happily growing up in. He studied the flora and fauna intently and regaled his mother with enthusiastic descriptions of his discoveries and observations. This delighted Lucy.

Over those years, Lucy invited to her home useful, knowledgeable and inspiring people to help mold and inspire Neil along the way. Many were the long heartfelt discussions with the brilliant people who came into contact with Lucy and

Neil. Neil listened intently to these discussions and absorbed as much knowledge as he could.

Lucy and Neil also did a great deal of traveling. They saw the world together, occasionally visiting his father for the obligatory short visit. Then they were off again to explore the world and all of its mysteries. Towards the end of Neil's seventh year, mother and son stayed for six months in India. It was a profoundly nourishing trip that filled the pair with a deep and abiding sense of well-being. The seeds for becoming a champion were planted in Neil during this time spent in this ancient place.

In the spiritual motherland of India, mother and son grew so close that nothing separated them. The internal and external boundaries that disconnect people or separate them completely dissolved between Lucy and Neil. They became essentially one person, sharing thoughts and feelings simultaneously. There was a flow of energy and ideas between them which allowed Lucy to pour herself into her son completely, giving him all that she had to give.

For Neil, his time in India was filled with subtle reminders of past expeditions as an earthbound human. Even at this young age, he had some sense of his past spiritual accomplishments. It was during this trip that Neil began calling his mother "maaji", an affectionate and respectful Hindi word for mother. Later when years had passed and he called her by this name one last time, Lucy's heart melted in the remembrance of this very sacred journey that they had shared together. This allowed her to leave this world in a state of bliss, so much had it meant to her.

During this trip to India, young Neil developed the ability to sense and even see the many benevolent beings who surrounded him and his mother. The open and imaginative minds of young children have always been able to more easily feel the presence of these helpers in spirit form. There are many names for them – angels, spirits, guardians and elementals. Many types of positive souls come to help humans embrace the light. They live in other realms of existence and on other planes of consciousness. Sometimes they are former loved ones who come back from time to time to give assistance through a difficult passage. For Neil, who was himself a highly developed soul with an important mission, there were a number of elevated souls accompanying him on his journey through this life. Unfortunately, he would not be able to feel their presence around him much longer.

It is essential for people to have natural and harmonious phases in their lives that allow them to connect to the divinity within them. It is also natural for evolved beings to want such periods to go on forever. But all phases must end in order to move onto something new. For Lucy, her exclusive time with Neil ended all too soon after they returned from India and shortly before Neil's eighth birthday.

8. The Viper Pit

Americans who rise from obscure poverty to high positions of wealth, fame and power know better than anyone else that what is presented as a climb to the pinnacle of success in our current system is really a fall into a deep, dark pit of vipers. The system as it now exists rewards people for being ruthless, for possessing a killer instinct, and for taking actions with no regard for consequences to themselves, others or the world to which they are connected. The system as it now exists punishes people for having a conscience, for being soft, generous and loving. Thus the system guarantees that no one will rise to a place of power unless they have first descended into the darkness of the viper pit.

The entire scaffolding of that society had been meticulously constructed by the Great Usurpers to bring out the lowest elements of the human being and to make sure that the lowest of the low became the highest of the high rulers with the power to dictate parameters and quality of human life for all. People of good faith and positive belief in the system who inadvertently gained entry into the upper echelon of wealth and power inevitably came to a harsh realization. They discovered that they were surrounded by venomous creatures. Not only that but as each creature possessed its own unique poison, the whole lot tended to be scared of one another and paranoid in general.

Being surrounded by venomous creatures was stressful. It made people feel like they were constantly under attack. It forced them to develop the aggressive and hostile aspects of their own personalities as a coping mechanism. After all, they could never relax; they always had to be in attack mode. They had to kill before they themselves were killed. They knew that the people below them wanted to supplant them and that the people above them would only keep them around for as long as they were of service. Once their usefulness had run its course, they might become dangerous upstarts who wanted their spot in the hierarchy and so must be crushed. In short, everyone was plotting against each other as a way of life. No one could let their guard down for even a minute. They may have found themselves being publicly destroyed by the media or vilified by what passed for the law in order that some higher up could fulfill a secret agenda. They might have been thrown under the bus just to provide a well-timed distraction on the evening news. The public looked on blankly while their whole world crumbled around them. The powerful were never safe. No one was ever safe.

Even if one of those powerful people had had a change of heart, they could not turn against the system and expose it for what it was. Each person had made a deal with the devil and there was no turning back. The families at the capstone of this pyramidal structure made sure that each significant person within the hierarchy had committed a crime or transgression or could appear to have done so in order that they be able to wield control over them. If any person turned against the system, the system easily devoured them using whatever dark information was available on that person as the fuel with which to roast them first.

The families at the top ran the media and law enforcement agencies. They owned the banks and controlled the money. It was their game and they had an overwhelmingly unfair advantage in playing it. No one on Earth could beat them at their very own game. The game was designed to play to the strengths of the malignant elite who, when they were not fighting each other, could come together in a moment to thwart a mutual enemy. The mutual enemy was usually connected to the teeming masses which through sheer force of numbers could, at any given moment, wake up and take down the despots who enslaved them. The despots knew this.

The Earth's current ruling class was aware of the law of attraction, of course. Everyone may have a different name for this phenomenon but the principle is always the same. Current leaders recognized that they were oppressing the masses. They worried that what they were doing would come back at them such that they would suffer the same fate they were inflicting on others. Every abuser worries about this. This group was no different.

Unfortunately most abusers do not use this worry about their misdeeds coming back at them to change their ways. In fact, the abuser mentality is built around the idea of keeping one's boot firmly on the throats of one's victims as a means of defense. There is a built-in program within any abuser that makes him dread what might happen if he were to lift his boot off of his victim's throat. Therefore, the abusive ruling class had worked for years to crush its many victims so thoroughly that they would never entertain so much as a passing thought of standing up and challenging them. It was for this reason that Adrian purposely moved at a measured rate to the top of the ruling class rather than mercurially. He took advantage of that time to use his inborn skills to make sure that any potential troublemakers he encountered along the way were completely beaten into submission. He prided himself on always working with the long view in mind.

In addition to his genetic programming and clear, conscious purpose in this world, Adrian had yet another unusual advantage that served him well as he worked his way up through the ranks to become king of the viper pit. The vipers were all being controlled by the Great Usurpers. During their past visits to the Earth, the Great Usurpers had schooled the earthbound humans who were devoted to them in the use of many kinds of binding secret rituals. Once these rituals and their uses were mastered to such an extent that their earthbound humans even knew how to pass them on to upcoming generations, the Great Usurpers then created with them a network of secret societies through which these Earth people could make frequent contact with their demonic extraterrestrial masters. It was in this way that certain earthbound humans were gradually transformed into "dark planners" for the Great Usurpers. The secret societies formed back then continued to function as planned in the present modern day era and their members secured positions of power in every major organization and government in the world. Once they were firmly implanted within the ruling class, the members of the secret societies wove their culture and its rituals and its vision for the future into the elite universities, into the political and financial institutions, into the arts and communication and many other places. Eventually the dark planners wove their symbology into every element of the modern earthbound human's experience.

With unswerving regularity, the powerful ruling class gathered in secret locations and performed their rituals, reaching out into the darkness and begging their demonic overloads to give them more wealth and more power. By voluntarily reaching out to the Great Usurpers and other demonic forces as they did, these people opened themselves up to being controlled by these dark forces and control them they did.

This dark system of contact through rituals and secret societies and meetings is what enabled the dark planners to continually seize ever more power and exert ever more control over humanity. They were getting their instructions and energy from powerful dark forces. In many cases, they were no more than puppets themselves being controlled like an avatar in a video game. Since they were being instructed from outside by what were essentially omniscient forces, there was very little need for these Earthly dark planners to generate any kind of complex conspiracies amongst themselves. When opportunities arose to move their agenda forward, everyone involved just knew what to do and did it. They all understood the evil game at their level of play and what they were supposed to do. They also understood the secret language each used to indicate their next move. Moving forward along the dark agenda had long since become nearly automatic.

Adrian's personal advantage in all of this was that he was born with a much deeper innate connection to the Great Usurpers than most of his associates. Plus he had their full attention and backing. He was not just better than the rest of the pawns at playing the game; he had been specially built for the game. By now the other players had been given orders to promote Adrian along the way so that he could reach the upper levels of the pyramid of power at the best possible time. Now that this was accomplished, he was to be a pivotal figure in the final stages of bringing humanity to its knees. It was at this time that his only son, Richard Neil, turned eight years old.

9. The Law of Intention

If it had been his choice, Adrian would have all but forgotten about his son and allowed Lucy to raise him indefinitely. He was consumed with carrying out his life's mission and deeply absorbed in the nuances of his accumulating wealth and power. Nothing else interested him. However, the unsettling thought that his work would ultimately fail unless he involved his son in it nagged at him. The thought persisted and strengthened over the years until Adrian could no longer ignore it. So it was that on Richard Neil's eighth birthday, Adrian stomped back into his son's life, grabbed the reins and took him away.

It is a little known fact that human beings have a thought force akin to the original thought that created the universe. Human beings who moan and wail in helplessness have no idea that within them resides a creative force that is almost identical to the creative force that was used by God to create the entire universe. This is why their begging prayers go unanswered by a deaf God. They already have the ultimate creative tool with which to not only pull themselves out of the abyss but with which they can create a divine existence within themselves.

When this potent thought force is focused into a clear beam of intention, the human creator will have his creation at some point. Adrian had the intention of creating an heir just as Lucy had the intention of lovingly raising a son. Lucy created a safe and loving bubble within which she was able to give all that she was and had to her son Neil. Once her intended work was essentially completed, Adrian burst that bubble, demanded his son back and began carrying out his intention of creating a despotic heir to his place in the evil hierarchy.

Once evolved beings learn to hone this near infinite creative force that resides within them, they become very powerful. When they can quiet their minds, develop a strong will force, and have a good understanding of the galactic laws that bind the universe together, they have the potential to manifest just about anything. Adrian had learned to use these skills in a destructive way just as Lucy had learned to use them in a creative and preservative way. However where Lucy had the backing of the natural universal powers and of divinity itself, Adrian had the advantage of not feeling constrained to play by the rules.

For instance, Adrian loathed being ill. With his association with the dark things of this world and the intensity of his malice and greed, he logically should already have been suffering from quite an assortment of physical maladies. However, he wasn't suffering physically at all because he automatically used his superior will force to push any potential sickness away from himself. This can be done by any evolved being who has the ability to focus their intent but with disease there is a catch. All illness is rooted in energetic patterns or thought forms which cannot be destroyed. They have to be expressed in some form by someone. So in cases like this where the pattern is being forcefully pushed away, that pattern typically latches on to close loved ones who either get sick themselves or have an accident of some sort.

Adrian's only "loved ones" were Lucy and Neil. During the first years of Neil's life, Lucy's protective bubble kept any of the gross energy that came from Adrian at bay. A bubble of love was easy for Lucy to create. She simply thought about and felt all the love that she had for Neil, for the natural world and for the Spirit Guides who visited her. When her heart was bursting with all of the love that she could feel, she placed an egg shaped sphere of that love around herself and her son.

This type of sphere is a very powerful protective force. Lucy and Neil could have thrived their whole lives within this bubble, quite oblivious to the harsh conditions dominating the Earth, had it not been for two factors. First as Adrian was Neil's father, he had a legitimate claim on his son. Secondly, it was Neil's destiny to experience working with both good and evil forces in this life and to finally make an irrevocable choice between the two. The script had to be followed. Lucy too had to follow the rules and allow Neil to step out of her bubble and be with his father.

Lucy could have continued to maintain the protective bubble around her son even when he was with Adrian. This would have ensured that Adrian's influence would only have had a superficial effect on Neil and not penetrated to the core of his being. But, alas, Lucy's enormous sadness at parting from her son left her scattered and vulnerable to the many negative forces that Adrian was willing away from himself. Once her guard was down, all manner of potential accidents and illnesses invaded Lucy with a fury. She became very ill and weak for what was to be a period of thirteen years. And in truth, she was never quite the same afterwards. It was during this long period of Lucy's weakness that Adrian exploited his opportunity to turn his son to the dark side.

10. From Neil to Richard

It is not very hard to corrupt and degrade a human being when the whole system of life on modern day Earth was so brilliantly designed to do just that. Doing nothing more elaborate than plugging a child into the mainstream system practically guaranteed that they would find their lowest vibrational frequency in a hurry.

Adrian's task was to suppress the "Neil" in his son while bringing out the "Richard". He already had a powerful tool at his disposal in the American culture that he was about to drop his son into. It was already set up to create Richards. Adrian did more than just submerge his son in American culture, however. True to form, he meticulously executed a carefully conceived plan to actually undo the years of his wife's loving work on their son. Step by step, he brought his innocent son to the doorway of the dark overlords whom Adrian served.

The modern day abusers who ruled the Earth had long had the ability to rationalize or spin their exploitation of others into a false reality in which they looked as if they were helping or even saving the people they were in reality abusing. Adrian was particularly expert at this. He was expert at sucking up the spiritual resources of others all the while creating the illusion that he was somehow sacrificing for his victims. His illusions were so deceptive that his victims often thanked him for his enslavement of them.

On some level Adrian knew that Lucy's poor health was due to her connection with him. He also knew that Neil's great love for his mother and her great love for him would be an obstacle to his turning Neil into the corporate despot he needed his heir to be. Therefore, he immediately imposed a separation on his marriage with Lucy, using her health and her needs as the stated excuse. In reality, a separation gave him the physical distance he needed from her to do his work on Neil. It also left their marital connection conveniently intact so that his negative energy could continue to flow into her, keeping Lucy sick and him strong. Maintaining an effective distance between Lucy and Neil ensured that Lucy would not be able to gather the strength to fight her husband off in order to protect her son from his contaminating ways.

Lucy was no ordinary hypnotized fool to just blindly fall for all of this without a clue. She was aware of what Adrian was doing even though she was a highly evolved, benevolent soul who generally paid little attention to the poisons and deceptions that circulated around her. However, the spirit that she had come to call her Divine Father began revealing more to her now than in previous contacts. Lucy was ready to hear more, she needed to hear more, and so he began sharing with her about the true nature of her mission on Earth. He transmitted to her the real scope of the conditions on Earth as well as the plans of the Celestial Fellowship for raising earthbound humanity to its now forgotten potential glory. He told her that Neil had to have this time with Adrian as it was an unavoidable part of the story. It was the dark part of the story. It represented one side of the conflict that Neil/Richard had to live through so that he could make his ultimate choice. Her son had to fully experience both sides, as painful as this would be to his loving mother. This was simply the way it had to be. So Lucy accepted it.

Adrian's first act, once he had separated Neil from his mother, was to convince him that his mother's poor health came in part from her having had to raise him. He planted subtle suggestions in his son's mind that Lucy did not want to live with her son any more. It was too much of a burden for her. This slow poisoning of Neil's mind against himself and his mother began to work its way into his little heart. Neil felt that he was a bad boy who had hurt his mother. He felt abandoned and unloved. He became fearful and angry. The dark and lonely conditions at his father's loveless mansions began to take their toll on him as well.

With each passing day, Neil's heart grew harder and

harder and his light continued to dim. His eight year old brain was going through a normal house cleaning period during which it was pruning synapses and rewiring itself. Old childhood memories and experiences began to fade from his view as did his knowledge and vision of the benevolent spirits who were accompanying him on his lifelong quest. He could no longer feel their support. His father's timing was impeccable. Neil was being reborn into a dark world which his father ruled unsympathetically.

A deep and violent rage began to grow in Neil. His father fed this rage with violent video games, toxic food and a restriction on loving contact of any kind. He prodded Neil into acting out in the private school he attended. Adrian demeaned the other students and teachers at the school which encouraged Neil to do the same. Adrian made his son believe that he was superior to everybody else at the school and everywhere else. He enrolled Neil in combat training and took him hunting regularly. He did not take him on the kind of hunting that takes skill and care but rather the kind of hunting rich people do which consists of shooting farm raised animals devoid of instincts and without a chance in the world. These coldblooded slaughters helped Adrian create a killer instinct in his son and a lust for blood. He methodically fed Neil's natural craving for love with materialism, rage, violence and malice. He surrounded him with all of the temptations that a decadent lifestyle had to offer. With unwavering attention to detail, Adrian slowly poisoned his son's heart and mind. Then, when the time was ripe, he prepared for a significant shift in Neil's training.

From time to time, after the reprogramming had moved far enough along and Neil was in his early teens, Adrian started taking his son with him to some of the occult rituals where the ruling families made sacrifices to their demonic overlords. It was at these rituals that Neil unknowingly first experienced contact with the Great Usurpers. By galactic law, more fully developed beings cannot just impose their will on lesser beings. Earthbound humans have to willingly reach out to either the Celestial Fellowship or the Great Usurpers. Of course, the Celestial Fellowship adheres more strictly to these rules than the Great Usurpers do. Nonetheless, even the Great Usurpers need people to make some movement towards them first before they can start using and abusing them.

So Adrian carefully brought his son to this point of making a movement towards them. Having been bombarded for years towards this end, Neil succumbed to his father's plans without fanfare. Although Neil was not allowed to participate in or even watch many of the more deviant rituals at the secret gatherings, his father deftly lured his son into taking an overt action towards his dark overlords.

Neil was fascinated by the large black statue of an owl always visible at these gatherings. He learned that it represented the hidden knowledge and wisdom that Adrian and his brethren, both past and present, secretly used and guarded. The brethren had also recorded all of the powerful knowledge that the Usurpers and even the Celestial Fellowship had shared with humans over the millennia and then developed parts of it into one curriculum after another of watered down versions of collective knowledge. These curricula were then strategically laced with religious superstitions and disinformation and then disseminated to the masses in powerful, culture changing ways. Century in and century out, the masses molded according to these curricula were kept powerless, flailing away at life with partial knowledge, incomplete tools and ineffective systems. When Neil learned of this, he was consumed from then on with having to know. He just had to open Pandora's Box. During a gathering sometime later, he approached the great owl and silently begged for the secret knowledge. He did not know it at the time but he was begging from the Great Usurpers.

Once Adrian's son had opened himself up this little bit to the Great Usurpers, they immediately attached four negative energetic entities to his being. Each entity radiated negative vibrations of anger, fear, hostility and malice 24 hours a day. This caused both him and the people around him to experience these negative feelings themselves, all of the time, for reasons they couldn't understand but eventually just accepted. The entities, in turn, fed on the dark energy of their unhappiness and grew ever stronger. A heavy condition of gross and disharmonic vibrations eventually surrounded Neil constantly.

By his mid-teenage years, Neil was overwhelmed by these dark forces. A deep hatred of God that was stored deep within him from long ago experiences during other lives on Earth resurfaced during this time of dark coaching in his life. When a person is fed with only hate and darkness, they adapt by learning how to draw energetic sustenance from these dark forces. They eventually end up trapped in darkness because with time they automatically become disgusted with all of the natural, loving forces that were designed to support them. They come to mistake poison as the real food. As a result, they inevitably create more hate and more malice in their environment which they themselves end up feeding on which only makes them more and more malevolent. Neil was at just such a tipping point. His father observed this and was pleased with how his son was developing.

In the early years, Adrian had never called his only child Neil but had only referred to him as "my son". At his instruction, his servants and the teachers and other students at school called him Richard, Rick and Rich – all names which Neil had loathed at first. Once the "Neil" in his son and his son's memory of his mother's love that had supported that side of him were nearly extinguished, once he saw an emerging hatred for the divine emanating from his son, Adrian began calling his son "Richard". It was then that his son, who could no longer detect any part of himself that had thrived during those first seven years in the bubble created by his mother's love, embraced the name of Richard and took it as his real name.

11. The Need for Upheavals

The Celestial Fellowship had long been encouraged by the resilience they saw in the people inhabiting Earth. Members of the Fellowship were very spiritually advanced and had developed the capacity to read the hidden mysteries behind creation. They nevertheless remained surprised by how much evil earthbound humans could create, indulge in and suffer and yet still remain relatively good natured in their daily lives. In observing how well earthbound humans stood up to the intense vibrational assault aimed at all levels of their beings by such negative entities, members of the Celestial Fellowship found that they had to rewrite their scientific and spiritual understanding of how much genetic and spiritual manipulation a soul-bearing being could withstand and yet still retain some element of their true nature. They also determined to find the hidden mechanism – the genetic component within the earthbound humans – that allowed them to withstand such an onslaught.

The resilience demonstrated by the people of Earth during this long, dark period was so marked that it would one day be recognized across the universe as a unique phenomenon. Elders across galaxies would cite it over and over again as a glowing example as they talked to their youngsters about resilience. That this resilience was an unexplained anomaly only heightened the universal fascination with this earthbound species. In many ways, in fact, the whole equation of earthbound humanity did not add up.

In the very distant past, the earthbound human population was begun on Earth by the introduction of a number of species of intelligent life, each of which was the result of a series of genetic experiments that had spanned thousands of years, had taken place in various locations around the universe and then had found their way to Earth by various means. Further experimentation continued after that on the Earth itself. Distant races, both positive and negative in nature, had had a hand in developing these species and populating the Earth with soul-bearing life. Some of the species flourished and even intermingled successfully. Some of them went awry, of course, and developed along divergent paths. Others rapidly went extinct altogether. More highly developed races from other parts of the galaxy came and went over time and they effected changes on many levels on the Earth. At times over the millennia, the evolving earth-bound human life on Earth was robust and clearly advancing while at other times it exhibited such downward tendencies that the resulting consequences nearly wiped them all out. During these times of contraction and destruction and massive loss of life, these souls that had by now become associated with Earth hovered around the planet waiting for a suitable opportunity to incarnate again so as to continue their spiritual journeys. Such opportunities always came around eventually within the rise and fall of earthbound humanity and the cycles of physical and energetic changes of the Earth itself.

Great Earthly civilizations rose, flourished, collapsed and disappeared even as planets near the Earth rose and fell too during this long time period. For instance Earth's sister planet, Venus, was rendered uninhabitable by the actions of the undeveloped and undisciplined soul-bearing life forms living on it. In their immaturity, they were reckless with their creative gifts and technologies with drastic, irreversible results. Some of the souls who had had to flee Venus ended up joining the Earth's populations so the collapse of Venus and other events of this type also contributed to the up's and down's of Earth's civilizations in significant ways.

From early on the Earth had been a meeting place, an experimental lab, a dumping ground, a galactic outpost. It had served many purposes over the millions of years. It was battled over and abandoned by turns for a host of reasons. With each turnover, the Earth was typically left with a fragment of a dying population. The fragments left behind typically had nothing to cling to but the crusty leftovers of its now collapsed civilization.

Finally after a very long period of unsuccessful colonization by various groups, the last of the great civilizations of this period on Earth collapsed. The giants living at that time began to die off. It was at this moment that the last of the major off-planet genetic "experiments" was dumped on this remote, abundant and yet tumultuous planet. This particular population was created in a distant solar system for specific reasons and surreptitiously spirited away to Earth, also for specific reasons. These new beings were left on Earth with none of the natural development and adaptation to its surroundings that come from ages of evolving in place as enjoyed by intelligent life everywhere. Rather they were a group of stranded, prisoner-like castoffs who had been bred to be warriors complete with an extremely heightened sense of fight or flight imprinted into their genetic code. They were abandoned on Earth and left to mix together with the locals and the remaining giants. This intermingling became the stock race for what became modern earthbound humanity.

Thousands of years passed during which it so happened that the Earth remained isolated from off-planet contact. This allowed the life forms on Earth to evolve according to the rules presiding on Earth without interference. Interesting progress was made. All of this changed, however, when the Great Usurpers discovered the Earth for themselves much in the same way that we now say that Christopher Columbus "discovered" America. Once the Great Usurpers set their sights on Earth and invaded it, they began intently extracting resources as well as tinkering around genetically with the Earthlings of that time in order to dumb them down. Alarmed at this negative development, intergalactic benefactors sent by the Celestial Fellowship came to Earth periodically and contributed their own higher genes to the earthbound humans' genetic pool. This embedded within the earthbound human genetic code a great deal of sleeper DNA that was spiritual in nature but which remained dormant under the conditions still dominating Earth. The Celestial Fellowship's plan was that this higher level genetic code would be activated at the right time in the distant future by a series of powerful catalytic events orchestrated to coincide with certain natural galactic and Earthly cycles. They felt that this approach would give the best possible chance for a spiritual awakening on Earth which would be supported by a necessary genetic mutation. All of this would allow earthbound humans of the future to expand into higher realms of consciousness.

As for the present, however, earthbound humans were a thrown together mess of many physical genetic races, both natural and experimental, with souls of various origins hooked in from all over the universe. It was with this unstable, unpredictable mixture of genetics and souls that the Great Usurpers had continued experimenting. It was with this unprecedented mix that they had found a way to pull life forms with the highest potential away from their inner world and outward toward a false, addictive, industrial, material world. The Usurpers had learned to poison the bodies, minds and environments of earthbound humans with corrosive chemicals, energies, and vibrational stimuli that were employed to make earthbound humans greedy, angry, fearful, and hopeless. The Usurpers had programmed them into passive slaves too helpless to liberate themselves from their predicament. Most debilitating of all, the Usurpers had skillfully hidden from them the truths about their origin and their Divine inner nature. They did this to ensure that the earthbound humans would remain disconnected from their infinite inner resources.

And yet, even with this checkered history and very foreboding present, the average earthbound humans were still reasonably benevolent in nature and wanted good things for themselves and their fellow beings. Their story was truly remarkable for the resilience and endurance it demonstrated. However, unbeknownst to them, the strength of these special qualities was soon to be put to the final test as the ultimate assault was about to begin.

Historically beings from other parts of the universe, in

compliance with the wishes of the Celestial Fellowship, had incarnated from time to time in human form and functioned as teachers with the hope of awakening mankind to its Divine inner nature. These interventions had not produced results that were as encouraging to the Fellowship as the discovery of earthbound human resilience had once been. In fact up to this point, the Celestial Fellowship had been rather discouraged by the great spiritual, technological and educational movements they had started on Earth. These movements usually started off well but time after time they were twisted by a few power-mongers into yet another force to be used to degrade humanity.

The lives and teachings of these higher developed beings were generally subjected to reinterpretion by many of the great religious texts and traditions so that only corrupted forms of the original messages still existed in human memory and culture. Nevertheless, these intergalactic missionaries did important work by introducing desirable spiritual qualities into the earthbound masses. They accomplished much.

By bringing with them their great spiritual accomplishments from other places, these intergalactic missionaries were able to incarnate at high levels on Earth and make profound contributions. Just by taking human form and living a spiritually advanced human life, they were able to raise humanity up as well as expand the possibilities of what spiritual heights human beings could hope to reach. Many of these higher developed souls also brought in with them very specific higher qualities and characteristics which went on to eventually become part of earthbound humans' genetic and spiritual makeup. Unfortunately, people did not easily assimilate these higher qualities. The collective slave consciousness and low self-esteem that were now fundamental to earthbound human life, both genetically and socially, blocked the human pathway toward higher spiritual approaches. As a result of this blockage, each significant movement towards what was spiritually higher that was started on Earth created great upheavals on the planet before these qualities could finally be integrated into the earthbound human system.

When trying to refine the vibratory level of an entire species, as well as that of the planet the species lives on, there are going to be side effects from the process. Transitions always trigger chaos and destabilization. You cannot solve a Rubik's Cube puzzle unless you spin the sides. You have to engage in a constant process of organizing, disorganizing and reorganizing the sides until all of the colors finally align. This disorganizing/reorganizing aspect of directed change is especially marked when earthbound humans have to integrate something new into their systems.

People experience the truth of this all of the time in their own families. A son or a daughter comes home from college. While away, they have integrated a new experience into their individual system that was outside of the family norm. When they come home on a visit or to live for a time, there can be confusion and even fireworks as their new perceptions and experiences are integrated into the family as a whole. Or it may be that the son or daughter wants to marry someone who is outside the caste, race or religion of their family. Whatever the new change is, the family has to undergo a process of integration that is often turbulent. Due to fear, prejudice, ignorance, or rigidity the family does not adopt the new way of thinking right away but instead resists it. Family chaos and upheavals ensue until the family is spun around on its axis and it finally embraces this new way of thinking or living. A new pattern of living emerges for the family and a period of stability follows.

That is a best case scenario, of course. Many times families shun the family member who is the change agent, leaving that family rigidly unchanged. However, if a shift does successfully occur, the pattern is as follows: introduction of the new paradigm; resistance to the new paradigm; stirring up of the family soup; and finally the new paradigm becomes a part of the family on every level.

As humans are multidimensional beings, these shifts

have to take place not only on the physical, emotional and mental planes but also on the spiritual, causal, cosmic and all other related planes of existence as well. New paradigms bring in new vibrational conditions to such an extent that all of the pre-existing vibratory conditions need to be either harmonized with the new one or let go. It is the blending of the new vibratory condition with the existing family structure/vibratory field that causes the upheavals. Without the help of insight, knowledge, and skills these adjustments tend to be full of upheaval, chaos and pain for earthbound humans.

If just one change taking place within a family can create such chaos, imagine the intensity of the chaos resulting from a change process that is affecting an entire country or the world as a whole. Earthly history is replete with examples of epic wars between good and evil, for instance, through which Divinity and its adversary of the time descended to Earth and waged war. The result of each of these epic wars was the bringing about of a spiritual transformation for humanity. Usually such changes were limited to bringing in a single spiritual quality for the human beings of that time such as devotion to God, compassion, or faith. For these incremental, singular changes to be made in the genetic and energetic structures of the human being, bloody wars and natural calamities, social unrest and dislocation, long pilgrimages, and changes in ways of daily life were the necessity and the side effects for thousands of years. Yet each of those movements represented just one necessary change, one blip on the radar screen of the necessary evolution of earthbound humanity. By contrast, the current epic movement of which Lucy and Adrian were a part will require a much larger, much more drastic transformational change which humanity will have to somehow endure and integrate. If Lucy's side triumphs, humanity will shift from the externalization of God to the internalization of God. It will represent the largest movement so far in human spiritual evolutionary history.

For this internalization to take hold in modern humans,

their vibrational condition will have to be severely reworked. The earthbound humans themselves will have to undergo a major genetic mutation just to be able to accommodate this new vibrational frequency. The genetic mutation will involve activating the significant percentage of sleeper DNA that the humans already possess. This process will change human beings so radically that the planet Earth will have to be restructured as well in order to facilitate and accommodate this change in the humans. In other words by the successful completion of this development, the whole planet and everything on it will have been tuned to a new, more refined vibrational frequency. The proposed change in frequency between the person of today and the person of a distant tomorrow will be greater than the gap that currently exists between the people of today and the one-celled amoeba. That is how radical this upcoming potential change was designed to be. On the other hand, if Adrian's side should triumph then the human being will be vibrationally reduced to the level of that amoeba and then stripped of its divine connection altogether. That also will be a drastic change.

This epic struggle will be like nothing humanity has seen or experienced before. No matter which side wins, the vibrational changes will reverberate throughout the galaxy and beyond. The upheavals and chaos that will be generated by the struggle itself and then the sheer magnitude of the shifts that will ensue – no matter which side prevails – will be unfathomable for the average person. World wars and atomic bombs will be unleashed. Large movements of the tectonic plates, erupting volcanoes, unimaginably powerful storms with three hundred mile per hour winds, major shifts in climate and weather, and the shifting of the Earth's magnetic poles will all change the physical Earth dramatically. Full conscious contact with both sides of the extraterrestrial teams battling for the soul of the planet will forever change the humans' conceptions about what the universe is and their role in it. Even human history itself will have to be completely rewritten to include all of the story that has been left in the shadows for so long.

According to the projection models of both sides, the human population will be reduced to a fraction of what it is now during this upcoming time of dramatic struggle and change. Those who survive will face nightmarishly harsh living conditions for some time. The humans' now legendary resilience will be put to its hardest test during that turbulent future. It will be a period of great suffering requiring enormous endurance, flexibility and faith. But if, through it all, the remaining people do manage to adapt and they take responsibility for their situation while consciously reaching up for guidance towards a more spiritual way of life, then the response from above will be so generous that earthbound humanity will be given all that it needs to evolve into what will essentially be an entirely new species.

12. Lucy's Ethyrical Farm

Even in her weakened condition, Lucy continued to converse with her spiritual benefactors and experience vivid dreams and visions. She could now see the great upheavals that were ahead for humanity. She knew that the collapse of earthbound humanity's civilization was imminent and unstoppable. Gradually it dawned on her that it would be imperative for humans to find a way to remember the old ways of living in order to have a chance at surviving the coming upheavals without being reduced to a state of starvation, destitution and worse. The large electromagnetic pulse that she had been warned about by her spiritual father would soon wipe out the electrical grid and most electronic devices in one sweeping knockout punch. This would take humanity back to at least the 1800's without the benefit of 1800 level skills, tools, knowledge, endurance and fortitude.

The Great Usurpers had been very intent that humanity must be coerced away from the land so thoroughly that their land-based, self-sufficiency skills and knowledge would completely fade away. They had calculated that once humans put down their tools and voluntarily locked themselves into narrow industrial slots, it would only take three generations of atrophy before they would forget how to survive naturally. History proved them right. The appropriators cemented in this degeneration by creating an enduring negative association with farm work, community-based work, husbandry, hand-crafting skills and hard physical labor in general. No one wanted to get their hands dirty any more. There was no way humanity was going to go back to the old ways spontaneously.

An easily hypnotized humanity had traded in its wealth of self-sufficiency and community work skills for a few highly specialized skills useful only within disconnected, consuming-oriented, machine-based, man-made activities. When that man-made system was eventually collapsed as planned, the people of Earth would only be able to beg and grovel in order to get their needs met. They would remember nothing of their inherent skills and knowledge and would actually be predisposed against such remembering. They would not recognize nature as a benefactor and would be predisposed against such recognition.

Lucy believed that there was still a chance for humanity to reconstruct some of the skills and knowledge that had been painstakingly developed over generations. She also knew that there were a few old-timers around with valuable knowledge and skills who longed to pass these gifts on to the next generation. There was also a great deal of this kind of information available on the internet as the ruling families had not yet closed down that method of sharing information. Between the advancing age of the last generation of skilled self-sufficiency people and the martial law she felt was approaching, Lucy realized that her window of opportunity for insuring that Neil would receive some of this vital training was closing all too quickly. Acting as swiftly as she could, she used the meager amount of energy she had left in her weak physical system to put together a year of training for her son.

At this time, Adrian was in the midst of bankrupting several countries so he did not care that Lucy took Richard out of school for a year. Adrian was at the top of his game and feeling invincible. Furthermore, he was so confident that Richard was now a younger version of himself that he did not worry that Lucy could possibly reverse his work of corrupting their son. Rather he figured that trying to deal with Richard would probably rob Lucy of any last bit of hope and vitality she might still have. Arrogance is so often the fatal flaw of the villain. It allows them to dismiss any possibility of their defeat. They place too much emphasis on paranoid delusions that could never really bring them down and yet scoff at the small and seemingly insignificant campaigns that usually result in their ultimate downfall.

Richard's sixteen year old hardened heart and hostile personality wanted no part of a year long visit with his mother during which he was supposed to learn about something as irrelevant as farming and handcrafts. The rhythm and condition of a naturally managed farm is very foreign and even threatening to the modern individual who is used to the chemical purity of a bleached modern world. Life on a natural farm moves much more slowly. Attention to detail is essential. Willingness to yield to the timing imposed by nature is critical. Richard had been so saturated by the deadening training he had received from TV, the internet, his cell phone and video games that he had no patience or tolerance for life on a farm. He was sure he would not be able to bear living in the unrefined, boring, outdated agrarian world. And yet, perhaps due to some inner compulsion, he went anyway. Modern adolescents often grumble and moan but go and experience what is new or different anyway in spite their outer protests, for deep inside they long for something to set them right.

Lucy never used force onced Richard arrived. Even though he was now physically on her farm, she knew in her heart that to truly bring her Neil back he would have to choose to come back. On the surface, Richard hated her. He no longer called her "maaji" but coldly spat out the word "mother" as only a rich, entitled, little punk can say it. Being called mother in this way sliced through Lucy's heart like a machete. Such wounds were hard to bear given her weakened physical condition but she bore his hostility day after day, prayed for him and waited patiently.

Lucy's farm was nestled in the Appalachian Mountains. She had been able to purchase it for a song shortly after graduating from college. As the years had passed, she had realized that her Mountains & Stars Farm was actually meant to be a haven or a retreat for others away from the many temptations and addictions that shaped and furnished the modern day world. More than that even, it was meant to become a place where people could contact the divinity within and gain a new approach to life. It was once she had recognized all of this that she had begun receiving instructions for developing her mountain farm in such a way that no damage would be done to the pure vibrational frequency that emanated from that special spot.

Thirty of the hundred or so wooded acres that made up Lucy's property were gradually developed into areas for cultivation and teaching and living space. Lucy was given what amounted to an internal instruction manual and operating system by her spiritual father for creating and maintaining her farm in the most effective, joyful, future oriented way possible. One day during meditation in her late twenties, she had experienced that the manual and operating system were suddenly downloaded into her. At the time she was not really aware of what she had received but over the years, she grew to appreciate it more and more as the new information and new approach to farming unfolded within her in a perfectly timed fashion. That "download" had been designed to change her consciousness in a very directed way. Soon enough it got so that when she needed to find a solution to some aspect of developing her farm, the answer usually bubbled up from within her. Whenever there was a time of confusion or special opportunity, she learned to make contact with devas and elementals on the etheric plane and ask for their special help. An answer was always forthcoming.

An important decision was made early on to keep the farm completely off the utility grid in order to protect the vibration of the property. Among other benefits this decision meant that no internet, computer, or TV intruded. All music was live, all stories were told from one heart to another. The small amount of electricity that was used on the farm came from an ingenious system of water powered generators that Lucy had built on one of her several spring fed ponds. The system worked very well. She could have easily built more of them and generated more electricity but as time went on and she learned new skills, she found that she hardly needed electricity at all so she didn't bother.

Over the years, Lucy also experimented with alternative construction techniques and drew to her farm the people with skills in those techniques who could come build structures on her farm. Her primary residence was one of the three light-filled earthships that had been built into a series of hills on the property. Thick earthen walls and sunlight streaming through the front windows into a very long, wide garden bed filled with a bountiful array of plants helped to keep her earthship warm in winter while those same thick earthen walls and that same enormous bed of indoor plants, along with large leafy trees outside the windows, helped to keep her home cool in the summer. To keep her food cool, she constructed a number of spring houses and root and fruit cellars using various systems that she experimented with. Although not as cold as a refrigerator, she discovered that these systems worked fine. She only needed to adjust her thinking a little on how to prepare, eat and store food for the whole system to work beautifully. The adjustments were all to the good anyway, she found, because they left her food with more vitality.

For water she had hand pumps built into several springs. Ponds, irrigation systems and rainwater catchment systems were constructed at strategic points all over the property as needed so that humans, plants and animals all had easy access to water. She had modest solar heated hot water tanks built next to the houses and she also used hot compost piles to heat water when she had large numbers of guests staying with her.

Lucy had long since mastered the art of cooking on a wood cook stove and used cook boxes and solar ovens to cook food naturally. To keep heat down in her kitchen in the summer, she learned to bake in an outdoor earth oven as well as cook meals in a fire pit she had built in a lovely location near the house. She really enjoyed cooking food in these ways and also enjoyed how much better the food tasted and felt both to herself and to her many guests. Just about everything else she needed for her simple life, she provided for herself by hand. Lucy had a full time farming staff to help her manage the farm and a small house staff to help with home management and hospitality for the many eager guests. As her health deteriorated, she relied more and more heavily on her staff who were like family to her and she to them. They loved working on Mountains & Stars Farm and with Lucy and felt very privileged. They all benefited from the time they spent there in terms of skill building and they evolved in more subtle ways as well from being immersed in the sublime spiritual atmosphere of the place with its special contacts with the plant and animal kingdoms and the higher planes of existence.

Even way back in college Lucy had learned that so-called modern day farming techniques wasted energy, depleted the soil of minerals and nutrients and eventually produced a weak kind of food or herb that was out of balance and low in nutrition. What she didn't know then was that for decades a special council within the Celestial Fellowship had been introducing plans and suggestions into the minds of open and gifted individuals for re-naturalizing the earthbound human food production system and re-vitalizing the food itself. Lucy was just happy to still be receiving new inspirations all of the time that contributed to a healing and renewing approach to the Earth and to food and medicine and flower production. Under the influence of this special council, she developed what she quietly came to call "ethyrical farming." This unique approach to farming was based in love and cooperation as well as innovative skills and knowledge. Lucy loved her farm and transmitted that love to all that grew upon it. She communicated with the devas and elementals on the etheric plane who were in charge of guiding the growth and animating the production of each plant form on Mountains & Stars Farm and followed their instructions as they came to her. At every turn she honored nature and the natural way of things. She offered love, high intention, and cooperation and received back an environment that practically shimmered with abundant growth, vitality, and soul-nourishing beauty.

Recognizing and using the natural contours of her land and working with the water flow from the top to the bottom of her hills, Lucy built haven after haven after terrace after micro-ecosystem after pond all along the way in which plant families flourished. Her farm was built as if Mother Nature herself had developed it to accommodate the natural elements and relationships of all that inhabited it. Once that infrastructure was established, Lucy studied the natural balance and symbiotic relationships between the plant families and animal life on her property. Over time she planted many, many types of plants and trees and bushes in order to attract the energy of many devas and elementals, thereby increasing the energy of the entire property. She planted her fruit trees and berry bushes with complementary plants that helped keep the soil strong and vital. She even sowed her seeds in an inspired, natural way. Every growing season, she filled buckets with seeds of over a hundred wisely chosen species of domesticated and wild plants, vegetables, culinary and medicinal herbs and flowers. Then she liberally spread her seed mix by the handful over her gardens. The seeds sprouted wherever it was best for them and grew happily within beneficial plant groupings. As she had done all of her life, Lucy sang, and prayed and hummed to her soil, seeds and plants bringing harmonious vibrations to them all. The devas and elementals loved these vibrations and her gardens were vibrant on all levels. Everyone and everything grew together – the plants, the animals, the human caretakers – and benefited.

When it was time to harvest, she and her assistants walked daily through the gardens and gathered heads of lettuce or handfuls of flowers and herbs, or basketsful of vegetables or berries whenever they were ready to be harvested. Lucy studied the animal pests that populated her area and learned what the ants, deer, mice, rabbits, raccoons and rats liked best to eat and then put those types of seeds in her bucket to be sown with everything else. In this way the pests generally left her produce alone as they preferred to eat their favorite delicacies instead. However as these pests still fertilized and irrigated the soil in the course of their travels, they became helpers in Lucy's grand design.

All of the rocks and boulders that were dug up while creating the gardens and ponds were buried next to fruit trees and left sticking halfway up in ponds. As the rocks were heated by the sun, they radiated that solar heat out into the gardens and the ponds, keeping them warm and extending the season in a natural, gentle way. The ponds also helped to keep the temperatures more consistent and warmer in the winter. Through such methods, Lucy was able to successfully grow fruits, berries and other delectables that normally did not thrive in her area.

The farm had a bounty of perennial plants happily thriving within their plant families, as well as many trees that provided edibles such as lindens and nut trees, heirloom apple trees, an Asian pear tree or two, as well as several plum and apricot trees. Many of these perennial plants and trees were growing together in harmonious permanent arrangements that came to be called food forests years later. Lucy's favorite trees were the many native persimmon and pawpaw trees she had planted back in her early twenties. Special Royal Lee cherries did not usually grow successfully in the mountains at all but her gardening system with the rock formations was so effective at keeping late frosts and unpredictable temperature fluctuations from killing the blossoms that her cherries produced abundantly year after year. She especially enjoyed these cherries and was known for her special recipes which featured them.

The farm had an ever growing assortment of both strawberries and berry bushes. For instance, many varieties of blueberries were grown to cover a range of harvest times and uses from jams to baked goods to dehydrated bursts of flavor for the middle of winter. Lucy's raspberries were like much of the rest of her produce – legendary in the area. The same was the case with the Mountains & Stars raw honey. Working in harmony with the gardens, food forests, fruit trees, and berry bushes were Lucy's seven humming bee hives which produced beautifully flavored natural honey and rich beeswax. Learning mostly from old timers in the mountains, Lucy learned about foraging as well. Her knowledge of wild plants grew to the point that she was eventually able to walk through the uncultivated acres of her farm and find nutrient dense wild foods pretty much year round.

Perhaps Lucy's favorite places on her farm were the areas she devoted to bamboo. She used bamboo in select spots on her farm to secure slopes as the bamboo rhizomes firmly held the soil together thereby preventing erosion. Carefully contained, harvested and managed, her various species of bamboo brought great bounty, utility, and beauty to her farm. There were areas on the farm, too, where tall bamboos grew freely. Lucy dearly loved to walk amongst the culms and listen blissfully to the leaves rustling in the wind. Bamboo had been brought to Earth long ago by beneficial beings who had intended for it to be used by the children of Earth as a generous and ever renewable resource. It was in this spirit that Lucy loved and appreciated it.

Rabbits lived in her three large underground green houses. They contributed body heat, fertilizer and innocence to her farm. The greenhouses were brilliantly constructed with a pit below the greenhouse which allowed cold air to fall off the plants in the winter and provided cool air flowing up in the summer. The windows of the greenhouses were recycled glass doors and were angled toward the sun just a foot above ground level.

A pair of draft horses hauled heavy timber and plowed out new garden beds. A donkey provided character, helped keep away predators and could also be pressed into service as a helpful pack animal from time to time. Her Great Pyrenees dog, Sampson, chased every coyote away from the farm with such vigor that few even dared come within a mile of the place and yet he was nothing but affectionate to the people who lived on and visited the farm.

Rare breed dairy animals were important members of the farm over the years. There was a small herd of Nigerian Dwarf goats whose kids brought much life and fun to the farm. Their milk made wonderful feta cheese and chèvre. The larger herd of

Dutch Belted family milk cows brought a calm stature to the pastures they grazed. The wise and gentle matron of the herd was Phoebe. Phoebe had calved a year earlier but was still giving about two gallons of milk a day which was a good amount of milk for a beginning milker to handle. Lucy planned to teach Richard how to milk Phoebe and how to make cheese, butter and kefir with the milk. She was also going to teach him the value of the manure from their wonderful, grass fed cows, both for enriching the soil and for use as a building material.

The milking barn was a unique modification of straw bale construction as was the large, airy hen house where Lucy kept her assortment of laying hens and a few roosters. Lucy favored a vegetarian diet for herself but found that she was often in need of the grounding that their eggs provided. Besides, the chickens with their complex social structure were very entertaining to watch and listen to. Along with chickens, Lucy had some guinea fowl which were also a source of entertainment and background noise. The chickens and the guineas were very effective at keeping the farm free of ticks, flies and other pesky insects. They were worth keeping just for that alone. However, the free ranging hens also scratched at the cow dung scattered across the fields, breaking it down so that it could fortify the pasture.

And this is how it was on Lucy's farm. Each life form performed multiple cooperative tasks for the farm that served all of its inhabitants. The bees pollinated the plant life and provided honey. The plant life provided fruit, vegetables and oxygen for all. The goats and cows provided milk, kept the pasture and other grasses and brush down and provided dung to help everything grow. Dung, leaves and rotting vegetation were mixed together to make compost so Lucy's garden soil was rich and potent. Lucy and her staff managed the farm by milking, planting, loving, feeding, pruning, singing, harvesting, praying and overseeing by turns. The devas and elementals gave spiritual guidance and added vibrational integrity to all of the life on the farm. Lucy also provided her love and guidance to all. Everything and everybody contributed to the wellbeing of the farm and each other. The many vibrations blended together into an uplifting, symphonic soul-satisfying, body-nourishing harmony. Lucy's spiritual guides filled her with love and a grace that flowed through her to everything and everyone else. All were valued and appreciated for what they naturally were.

Lucy's Mountains & Stars Farm had been open to serve the community for years. Her abundant fruits, herbs and vegetables were sold at farmers markets as well as donated to local schools, shelters, families and neighbors. Local schools and homeschools brought their children on field trips so that they could begin to learn to milk, and to harvest and process food. Old time retired farmers and crafts people were available to provide training and do demonstrations from time to time. Older children and young people worked in apprenticeships that Lucy set up which changed lives over and over again. After years of this collective work, there wasn't a child within 25 miles of Lucy's farm who did not know how to milk a cow, establish a garden, talk to a fairy or deva, churn some butter or prune a fruit tree. There wasn't a child who hadn't experienced Nature as their support, teacher and partner.

Richard, however, was a young man who did not like it at the farm and was uncomfortable there. He did have faint memories of the time he and his mother had shared at the farm years ago when he was a small boy. Part of him could not bear the pain of seeing how much the farm had blossomed without him. On a more conscious level, though, he looked down on all the people, animals, tools, lifestyle, dirt and runaway plant life. He felt that this was a barbaric and unnecessary way to live and he wanted no part of it. All that he had with him as an escape from this hell was a small hand held video game. He played it constantly. Without saying anything, Lucy waited patiently for it to run out of batteries. Richard's cell phone did not get a signal at the farm and there was no wifi available for him. With no electrical outlets or computers to recharge it, the phone also ran out of life as well. It was then when the video game and phone were reduced to inert packaging that Richard had to face himself.

Within every human being there exists a farmer. Since their arrival on Earth, except for the periods dominated by grand civilizations that had inevitably imploded and disappeared, earthbound humans had spent most of their time living in small family-based or tribal-based agrarian groupings or villages gathering and growing food. Farming was deeply rooted within the DNA of every human. So for Richard it was only a matter of time before his mother's farm pulled the inner farmer out of him.

Richard was actually not a lazy or passive person. He had a strong, healthy body and a keen, active mind. When deprived of any other way out, it did not take long for him to shake off the stupor created by the haze of TV, video games, internet and electrical poisoning. As Richard possessed his father's qualities of ambition and a strong will as well as his mother's artistic nature and unflagging perseverance, it was not long before Richard's pledge to mope around the farm until his visit with his mother was over broke under the soul-crushing boredom that was torturing him. Slowly, he began to participate on the farm.

He did not take to it at first as his attention span had been so weakened by modern life that he could not stay consciously aware throughout a whole farming activity. He learned the physical skill of milking well enough, for instance, but could only get halfway through a milking session before he became distracted and his hands grew tired. He had the same experience gardening, scything grass or churning butter. He started out okay but soon grew restless and bored. He had not yet developed the inner reserves of endurance he needed to complete these tasks. However, he did have a competitive streak a mile wide so even though he did not think much of farm work, he could not allow it to beat him either.

Gradually Richard began to master a number of skills. The vibrations at the farm and the vibrations of the modern day world were so drastically different that it had taken him a while to get into harmony with the rhythm and flow there. As he did, though, the skills came to him more easily. He had no conscious desire to be in harmony with this ecosystem but as time passed, it just sort of happened.

Richard was stubborn, though, and the wounds that his father had inflicted on him and the malevolence he had cultivated in him would not go away from one visit to a farm, no matter how nurturing it might be. So Richard continued to hold to the position that he looked down on farm work. Therefore he could not allow himself to make contact with the etheric plane that was available to him there or be proud of his physical accomplishments. Nor did he acknowledge to himself or anyone else – particularly his mother – that he was actually enjoying farm life. But he was dimly aware that he was expanding and becoming more of a human being. He was aware that he was expressing parts of his inner world that needed to be expressed. There were files and programs in his inner system that were being called up and used by this life on his mother's farm. His system was functioning on a higher level, in a more complete and balanced way. There were things about the farm life that filled him with a deep sense of well-being. A part of himself that he did not readily acknowledge was whispering to him, "Yes this is right. This is the way it is supposed to be." And then it was over.

Before he knew it, Richard's year at his mother's farm came to an end. Lucy had put so much energy into praying and energetically propping her son up through his transition back to a more natural life that her health had begun to decline again. She was upset by this because although Richard did not give her even a hint that the experience was having a positive effect on him, Lucy could sense that she was really close to seeing a breakthrough in her son. However, her health was collapsing and Adrian had turned his attention back on Richard and was calling him back.

It was heartbreaking for Lucy to part with her son again,

especially since she knew that she had been so close to bringing him back to her. However, she also sensed that he had gotten enough of what was necessary to keep the Celestial Fellowship in the game. Richard hardened himself again as he dressed neatly in his fancy clothes. He put on the appearance of a kid who was getting out of a juvenile detention center and heading back to the world he loved. Even in parting he did not want to relent and give his mother any indication that he had softened. He gave his mother a quick, stiff hug and quickly pulled away as he made his exit. Lucy held him there for just a moment. She could see that his eyes were soft and watering. She breathed a sigh of relief as she thought to herself, "Ah, there's my Neil."

13. The Law of Allowance

The war-oriented model of socialization that now dominated planet Earth did not allow for words like "surrender" or
give any credence to phrases like "Let it be," or "It is out of my
control." "Surrender" was a word Americans particularly loathed
and in this way Adrian was very American.

Abusers often believe that they are actually valiant heroes. In their narratives, their horrible actions are always justi-
fied. They blame their victims for forcing them into their abusive
actions. As far as they are concerned, they are only giving their
victims what is deserved so it is really the victims who are responsible for whatever the abuser is doing to them. Facing the
truth about what they really are and what they are really doing
is like kryptonite to abusers so abusers are driven to suppress the
truth at all costs. They exert power and control over every situation so that they will not be destroyed by the truth slowly seep-
ing out and eventually engulfing them. If they were to let events
run their natural course, then the truth would inevitably surface
and the abusers would be shown up for what they really are.
Their illusion would be destroyed. In reality the truth is always
there to be seen so abusers have to put blinders and strangle-
holds on their victims in order to prevent them from seeing what
is happening and speaking the truth themselves. Therefore abusers seek to control the narratives about all of the events going on
around them. "Surrender," or "going with the flow," are just not
options.

Unnatural patterns of abusive dynamics and dishonest
narratives did not arise naturally in the course of the evolution
of earthbound humans. In fact, such patterns are unwanted on
the soul level by earthbound humans or anyone else. Rather, the
abusive characteristics and compulsions that now plagued earthbound humanity had come as a result of an ancient mistake that
had twisted and proliferated into what had become the modern
people who had overrun the Earth. From a larger perspective,

the "abuse" of modern times was a form of warfare taking place on the battlefield of human relationships. It was the use of tactics, strategies, deceits, threats, bribes, separation and isolation, coercion and, most of all, force in the field of relationships which are meant to be governed by love. This malefic approach to life could be traced back to the injection of the genetics of a war-centered race that had tipped the scales of an already ravaged earthbound population towards abuse.

Many ages ago on a distant planet far from Earth, there had been an advanced race of people who had wanted to evolve into a more peaceful race so they genetically modified themselves to remove any aggressive tendencies from their genetic code. This worked for them very effectively at first. Interpersonal conflict disappeared and the progress that flows from peace and harmony blossomed. They initially experienced great revelations in the field of spirituality as well. However, an aggressive race from another corner of the galaxy eventually discovered and began looting these peaceful people. The word went out and in fairly short order, that peaceful race enjoyed peace no more. Having unbalanced themselves with their genetic manipulations, they had unwittingly created a situation that actually drew to their planet races equally unbalanced in the opposite hostile, aggressive, insatiable direction and against whom they now had no defense.

In a panic, the people realized that they would be forever at the mercy of any aggressive race who could reach their planet through space travel. They were unwilling to give up their pacifist way of life by reincorporating aggression back into their genetic code. Instead they decided to use their skill at genetic experimentation to create a race of humanoids somewhat similar to themselves but with much more aggressive tendencies. They substantially heightened the level of the flight or fight response in their made-to-order soldiers so that they would be very aggressive and drawn to combat. They shortened their lifespan in order to pull for intense, vigorous lives and diminish the possibility of any transmission of knowledge or wisdom from one generation to the next. They decreased the intellectual level of their soon-to-be army. This ensured that the pacifists would always remain at least one step ahead of their newly created slave race.

As they went along working with their new creations and learning to live with them, the pacifists found makeshift ways to maintain social control over them. Going by memory, the pacifist masters designed and manufactured the weapons their soldiers used. They also developed extensive computer programs to train their newly created warrior slaves in necessary military maneuvers and protocol. They provided generously for all of their soldiers' needs of daily life including food, housing, clothing, entertainment, technology and medical care. Everything the pacifists could think of as appropriate was provided for their newly created army. Meanwhile, they made sure that their soldiers' activities were limited to the tasks specific to soldiering relieved only by occasional stints of related simple labor. As masters, the pacifists did not share with their slave soldiers any information about God, about the purpose of life or about universal, natural laws and they never, ever breathed a word to their slave soldiers about their origins.

Nevertheless, in time this peaceful people discovered that they had overshot their mark. While the genetically engineered soldiers were excellent for quite some time at repelling marauders, new problems arose. The result of their genetic tinkering turned out to be a race so hostile and belligerent that they were almost impossible to control. The soldiers resisted following orders, resisted cooperating even with each other and just generally exasperated their passive slave masters at every turn. Even worse, the soldiers' propensity for fighting was so great that they fought with everybody. They fought with invading marauders, but they fought with each other constantly too, even during critical battles against invading forces. It would only be a matter of time before they turned and fought their pacifist masters as well.

Baffled by the outcome of their impulsive work and lacking the grit to exterminate the wayward experiment themselves, the passive ruling class of the planet looked for an off-planet place to bury their problem. They searched the galaxy and found a remote planet on the outskirts that looked biologically suitable as a place for their soldiers to inhabit. It also had the necessary advantage of being what they thought was an unknown and unnoticed little planet. So this advanced race transported and then stashed their unruly "mistake" on this small planet and washed their hands of the whole nightmarish situation. The fact that the problem was caused in its entirety by their impulsive attempt at balancing or improving themselves artificially didn't make them pause in their considerations at this point at all. It didn't occur to them that marooning their disgraced warriors on an unknown planet in a remote corner of the galaxy might also create further unintended consequences.

So the genetically engineered, hostile, soldier type people were unceremoniously dumped on Earth. They did not bring with them any of what is typically necessary for such situations such as knowledge about who they were or where they came from. They did not bring skills for assessing and adapting to new situations, or even basic life skills. They had no way to put a new life together or chart a reasonable course towards the future. As time passed, the soldier race interbred with the mixed races already existing on Earth from previous experiments. Interbreeding allowed them to survive but without any real sense of purpose governing their survival. Without the genetic and spiritual modifications that come from a long, natural evolution, the aggressive tendencies of the soldier race overwhelmed everything and finally metastasized into the uncontrolled and unregulated species that came to dominate the planet. Unreceptive to guidance from higher beings, this new species spread without the loving guidance that is necessary for soul-bearing beings that have near-infinite capacities to create, preserve and destroy but otherwise little internal development.

After many failed civilizations over many thousands of

years, the Earthmen were finally considered a failed experiment by the wise and benevolent council members who governed the Celestial Fellowship. The Entrusted Ones met to determine how they could best assist righting this genetic ship, so to speak. After careful consideration, the benevolent brotherhood yielded to the less than palatable choice of allowing more genetic experimentation on the earthbound humans – but this time under their own very careful supervision. The hope was that the proposed genetic alterations would elevate the people of Earth enough to enable them to one day step into full galactic citizenship. So over a long ensuing span of time, highly developed beings came down to Earth and introduced their more evolved DNA into the earthbound humans' genetic pool. This did eventually have the hoped for salutary effect. Earthbound humans were able to shed many aggressive tendencies through this painstaking process and become more intelligent, more spiritually balanced beings.

There was a serious consequence to this choice of pursuing genetic enhancement, however. By opening the door to genetic experimentation, not only were the benevolent beings allowed to experiment with the earthbound humans in order to achieve a higher goal but the Great Usurpers and other hostile beings were able to continue their experiments with them as well in order to achieve their nefarious goals. Only now their experiments could be more out in the open. They were no longer constrained by the fear of being caught at carrying out unauthorized genetic manipulations of a species.

After eons of time and many routes taken towards genetic enhancement, there came to be roughly three distinct groups of humans on the Earth. The first group was comprised of people who had started to evolve and had found some balance between the spiritual and material sides of themselves. The second group could only be described as human sheep. They were generally passive and more than willing to follow orders from the powers that be, whether for good or bad. This group had descended from those who had been bred to be slaves for the dominant races who had gorged themselves on the Earth's resources in the distant past. While this group of earthbound humans was passive and compliant most of the time, they could also become irrationally aggressive when sufficiently provoked and turn into a violent, uncontrollable mob. The third group of humans had evolved intellectually but had not moved forward either spiritually or in their character development. They had acquired more highly developed mental and analytical abilities but they had still retained the hostile and aggressive emotional tendencies that had come down from the genetically engineered soldier race from the faraway planet. This group of people also maintained a deep paranoid fear that they would once again be subjugated. This unconscious fear was rooted in their ancestral memories of being abused slaves. As a consequence, they had developed a lust for power and a thirst for wealth as stepping stones toward their desire to become the new controllers of the planet.

As the humans in the first group were still like kindergarteners in waking up to their spiritual reality, they did not have the necessary skill and experience to become the steady leaders of vision the earthbound humans needed at this point. Also many in the first group had had past experiences like Richard of having been tyrants and despots in past lives. They had been a part of the third group back then before they had developed some spiritual maturity. These tendencies from their pasts as abusive leaders invariably came back up and expressed themselves when these now more spiritually centered people gained some status and position in the present world. Echoes of lust for power and control or a tendency to become overwhelmed by the demands of the masses often caused the members of this group to regress and fall back into negative propensities and emotions. Often their former despotic ways were revived and they experienced a spiritual fall. As a result, the number of humans in this group tended to rise and fall over time. Attempts at leadership came and went as a consequence.

Leadership potential in the other groups was mixed.

The second group did not have the genetic qualities to become leaders at all. The third group was another matter altogether. This group knew who they were and had had years of experience in seizing power and control from their brother and sister human beings. With their new found intelligence and the help and direction of the Great Usurpers, this group had developed complex destructive weapons and powerful systems of social control. They had enormous drive and the organizational ability to use both but did not have the maturity or spiritual capacity to handle either responsibly. Thus the Earth was dominated by these genetically modified aggressive beings who possessed neither conscience nor compassion but who did possess weapons capable of destabilizing the universe.

It was a fact of life that the leaders of the third group could not relent or take their feet off of the throats of their victims ever. If they did, humans would evolve and along the way they would naturally embrace their new found genetic capacity for wisdom and spirituality under the gentle guidance the Celestial Fellowship. If such an evolution took place, the third group would soon go extinct. Being hostile and aggressive is like being a sharp rock that sticks up out of the ground. The rock is menacing at first but nature has ways of smoothing everything out. The wind, rain and sun slowly wear away the rock's sharp edges until it becomes a rounded part of the larger harmonic system. Aggressive beings who are self-destructive by nature do not have a long shelf life. On some level they know this. This adds to their paranoia and leads to the development of even more aggressive and impulsive behaviors by which they desperately try to hold onto the power and control they have so far secured. The leaders of this group had been building power and control over thousands of years. To accomplish this they had developed a very heavy handed approach toward the world. They had long manipulated and forced their will on everyone and everything. Their way went in the opposite direction of the natural path but unless they had complete control over their world, they would be reabsorbed back into the natural order.

The history of the Earth has long been checkered by cycles of abuse. Over the millennia, earthbound humans built civilizations and cultures sometimes influenced by the Celestial Fellowship and sometimes influenced by the Great Usurpers. Most of the time, they were influenced by both groups at the same time which further deepened the confusion and the struggle. There were ups and downs and highs and lows to each one of these many movements on the Earth but they all ended in pretty much the same way – with the earthbound human civilization completely collapsing. Then after some time and even terraforming managed by higher developed extraterrestrials if necessary, the Earth would recover and life and humans could thrive on it once again. Then the whole experiment would start over again, giving the many souls bound to this planet the opportunity to once again start incarnating here in order to work free of their bondage.

A complete fresh start on all levels is not possible, however. The many souls that are bound to an earthly life may start over with a new life in a new body on a fresh Earth but they still come with past impressions, tendencies and uncompleted work from their former lives imprinted on them from the soul level right down to the cellular level. This fact holds true for individuals as well as the cohorts of those who incarnate together. Even after the several times that the Earth had been wiped completely clean of earthbound humans and then repopulated by a somewhat upgraded human model, those incarnating souls still had their same spiritual baggage to deal with.

The Great Usurpers found that with just a little effort it was always pretty easy to corrupt the new species of earthbound humans and get them to repeat their same abusive cycles all over again. They learned that the most powerful tool for keeping these negative cycles going was for them to dominate and control the economic and social structures that developed each time on Earth. It really only took a slight shove to get the people of Earth to make the same bad choices anyway. But no matter how easy it appeared to be to push each version of earthbound humans towards the negative, the Great Usurpers never allowed themselves to forget that eventually the soul-bearing people of Earth would learn from their mistakes and develop an aversion to all of the pitfalls and substances and tricks that the Great Usurpers had used to bring them down time and time again. So the Usurpers and their minions, the dark lords, kept a tight grip on any human access to information about the history, origin and true spiritual nature of earthbound humans. Near total control was critical.

It was for exactly this reason that Adrian had awakened one day at the end of Richard's year away to the realization that he had allowed his contact with him to be broken for too long. He sensed that if he did not bring Richard back under his control immediately then nature would start to run its course and Richard would likely embrace his divine inner qualities, as this is what was supported by nature. Wasting no time, Adrian contacted Lucy and demanded that his son be returned to him without delay. It was time that he refocused his attention on Richard's grooming.

Unlike Adrian, Lucy was fully able to surrender to the law of allowance. She knew that the creative and positive forces in the universe would eventually draw everyone and everything back to the Source anyway. Good earthbound humans were willingly working their way back home, at least most of the time. Bad earthbound humans were just like an angry toddler in the corner having a tantrum for a while before running back and sitting on his mother's lap. Lucy knew that her love for Neil was a more compelling and a longer lasting force than Richard's – Neil's alter ego – remaining desire for power.

So as difficult as it was for her emotionally, Lucy allowed her Neil to return to his father even though he would again suffer the effects of Adrian's dark ways. It was only her faith in the natural order and in the inevitable ascension of the earthbound human being to a higher vibrational state that allowed her to submit to this abomination. However, Adrian could not allow in any way, shape or form for Richard's soul to follow its natural path back to its original source. In the same way, Lucy's farm had been created in full reliance on the natural world while Adrian's world was an ordered one in which he had to control everything and everyone around him. Adrian's whole existence was dominated by being controlled by the Great Usurpers and being in control of the earthbound humans.

Being controlled by a demonic puppet master's strings is the ultimate curse that all abusers suffer from. They can't let their guard down either inside of or outside of themselves for even a minute. They have to crush any connection or guidance that might well up from within. They cannot afford to develop a rich inner world or become a vibrant person who feels, explores, loves and emotes. In the outer world, they cannot let anyone else's views, feelings, needs or personality hold sway in their lives and influence their decision making. Adrian embodied all of this. He was a compulsive, controlled automaton that followed a strict set of rules and compulsively followed orders minute by minute, day after day. Nothing was left to chance. Everything was in complete, uncompromising order. He just ran a nail around a circular track, over and over, carving the groove deeper and deeper so that everything in his life followed that one groove, willing or not.

This was a core difference between Lucy and Adrian and, in fact, a core difference between good and evil. When they are being good, good people follow the universal rules. They live disciplined lives in service to God and in complete harmony with His natural creation in all of its manifestations. They climb a very narrow path of righteousness and connectivity. Their loving hearts long to reunite them with their beloved Father. This Divine craving is the beacon that guides them home. They may deviate from the path from time to time or temporarily lose sight of their goal out of self-doubt and other weaknesses but they always find it again. They gladly return to their eternal pathway and go dancing along it because they have made their choice to return to their eternal home. To succeed, they have only one option, one narrow path to follow with no apparent freedom, but within that one option all of the unlimited resources and capabilities that exist in an infinite universe are fully open to them.

On the other hand, Adrian and evil beings like him have what appears to be enormous freedom to indulge and break the rules at every turn. And they exercise that freedom fully. They have an infinite number of deviant choices and pathways from which they can choose. They are free to exploit and manipulate the universe around them and they do so. But with each choice they make that deviates from the Divine path, they automatically activate the powerful Divine laws and forces that exist to bring them back to the higher road. The reality, then, is that the outcomes and consequences of their poor choices ultimately have the effect of pulling them back towards the natural current that is working its way back to the Source. To hold off this gravitational pull towards the good of their wayward and interfering actions, the evil ones designed compulsive and ritualistic behaviors as a check against the Divine laws and forces. In the end, they too have given up their freedom as they engage in these compulsive and ritualistic behaviors without choice or deviation so that they can remain stagnant in an ever changing universe. They have given up their freedom in order to willfully choose to forget the natural order and their connection to God.

So both Lucy and Adrian had given up their freedom of choice. Lucy and souls like her were on the path of voluntarily giving up their individuality so as to merge back into the infinite whole. Lucy was not free in the conventional sense as she was a servant of the Divine Will that governs the known universes and by whom she was guided both firmly and lovingly in every aspect of her existence. Adrian and the souls like him who had apparent unrestricted freedom to do whatever they wanted whenever they wanted could not be called servants. Rather they were slaves to their misbegotten desires. He and the beings like him exercised their option of freedom of choice but in doing so, they were bound to cyclically repeat those choices. They would live variations of those same lives time and time again until they were extricated from the web of their own creation and found themselves back at the narrow path that would lead them home to their Creator. Neither was free. One served voluntarily; the other was a slave to their own choices. One accepted their fate; the other resisted it. That was another of the simple and seem-ingly small differences between these two oppositional forces that were battling it out in this epic and had battled it out in all of the epics that had come before and those that may come afterwards.

14. Richard's Prison

For the first few weeks back at his father's mansion, Richard continued to wake up at sunrise to dress and go out to the barn and milk Phoebe. Somewhere between his bed and his bedroom door, though, he would come back to his surroundings with a start and realize that he was no longer at his mother's farm. No, he was back home in the city now. With mixed feelings, Richard would go back to bed for a few more hours of restless sleep.

As time wore on, it gradually dawned on Richard that he couldn't really say that he was at home exactly in this mansion of his father's. It was more that he was in an unrelenting prison that was suffocating him. At times he felt like he couldn't bear to stay there another day while at other times, the days just slipped by. But just as had been the case at his mother's farm, boredom overtook him. The act of shaking off the boredom led him to eventually embrace his surroundings which, in turn, drew him back into the darkness.

The modern earthbound humans' current system of enslavement was perfectly designed for them. No matter what New Year's resolutions they might make, their addictions were always right there waiting for that moment of weakness to pull them back into the abyss. This was no less the case with Richard. The contrast so fresh in his mind between his mother's farm and his father's mansion allowed him to see how heavy and unnatural his lifestyle was at his father's mansion. In fact at first the food, the video games, the music, his peers and even his clothes there repelled him. They all left a bad taste in his mouth as if they were poisonous. But all of those things did not go away. Instead they just waited for him to come back to them.

Before long he needed something to do. The activities that had enslaved him before were still all that were available to him. So one day he idly picked up a game controller and started blowing things up on a screen. A week later he went back to the processed foods and toxic beverages. The chemical-based products and furnishings in his father's mansion also started to wear on him as did the cold and lifeless vibrational condition that enveloped the place. In a short time, the faint glimmer of light that had started to reemerge from Richard's heart while he had been staying at his mother's farm began to fade.

With each step back into the modern system of life and conquest, another layer of grossness wrapped around his heart like a cocoon. Soon he could feel nothing. He became dim, hostile, and unresponsive to the world around him. He went back to being one of the many human bumper cars that banged around without feeling a thing. He became like so many family members in the so-called developed world, the machine-based world, who are self-contained in their own pod, watching their own TV, playing on their own computer, talking on their own cell phone – each oblivious to the desperate state of the other family members with whom they shared blood ties. He was just like so many who shared geographic and community-based ties and yet only made restricted connections with each other through mechanical interface devices which impeded and monitored their communications and connections with their fellow beings.

For Richard it was painless and painful at the same time. He passively allowed himself to be closed off from the world. He went numb so that he wouldn't feel the pain. But the pain was buried deep inside of him waiting to reemerge once again from the depths of his heart. It was exactly this pain, this desperate longing to reunite with the inner, eternal Beloved that through the ages had made human beings strive to become what they were meant to become. It was exactly this pain that was the seed of hope for Richard.

15. Adrian's Repetitive Behaviors

Obviously not in a position to trust their fate to the natural laws governing the Earth, Adrian and his ilk twisted those laws in a way that allowed them to create contrary laws and cycles that supported their dark ambitions. This was principally accomplished by repeating the same necessary lies over and over again, in the same way over and over again, for century after century after century. With each repetition, the lies gained power and strength. More and more people absorbed the lies and then repeated them themselves through their own words, thoughts and deeds. On and on the lies snowballed. Eventually, the body of lies became so big and so powerful that it became an energetic body in its own right with its own gravitational field.

This was how the dark leaders of the planet Earth were able to keep things from slipping out of their control. They simply cast the same spells over and over again by telling the same lies over and over again until their webs of deception created nearly impenetrable barriers to change. The dark leaders were able to keep the continuity of this work intact by carefully executing their plan slowly over centuries. Within secret societies, they used initiations and rituals to indoctrinate their new members, generation by generation. They maintained a shared understanding that new members were reincarnations of past members who had returned to further the work and would return again and again into the endless future to further that same work.

The power and the continuity of the work were further enhanced through carefully planned breeding. Only certain families were allowed to intermarry and provide progeny. The great care with which this practice was maintained over the centuries assured them that the Great Usurper portion of their genetic makeup remained strong. They experimented for years with selective breeding among themselves and now believed that they had created a superior race that was fit to rule the world. They referred to the mass of other people who shared the planet as "useless eaters" and thought of them as nothing more than livestock. The dark planners kept their genetic pool isolated and insulated from the livestock and kept their souls reincarnating into these same families to build momentum over time.

With such a long view, members of the secret societies and their families did not need to see the fruits of their labor in their current lives. They just methodically carried out the slow roll out of compulsive and repetitive behaviors which allowed the illusions and webs to grow bit by bit over time. This unusual characteristic was an important key to their success. Most people feel compelled to complete their work in one life and so feel under the gun for much of their lives. This can make them prone to making mistakes or rushing the work. After all, their work has to be accomplished within a limited forty years or so. The puppet masters that ruled the Earth from the shadows were not under such restrictions, however, so they could work slowly from generation to generation with a continuity of both actions and players. The dark ones had an enormous advantage in being able to do their work for one lifetime, dying, reincarnating back into the same closed community and picking up where they left off in their next life.

After centuries of this cyclical pattern, their dark conspiracies were now finally emerging from the shadows and rising into the crescendo of a planetary takeover. At this point, it appeared impossible that the rest of the earthbound human population could wake up and stop this madness. The dark planners' cumulative work would finally have its full expression.

This method of control by webs of lies employed by the minions of the Great Usurpers required a great deal of concentration from them and a consistently dysfunctional use of resources. For centuries the powerful families of the secret societies had repeated the same lies over and over again regardless of what the universe threw back at them. If the villagers were shouting the truth back at their lords and kings, the lords and kings only calmly repeated their lies over and over again back at them. If nature produced results that could easily be interpreted as warnings to these leaders to stop their destructive actions, the leaders only continued to repeat their same lies over and over again. The members of the secret societies steadfastly ignored everything but their own lies. They held so tightly to their lies through centuries of unbroken recitation of them that eventually these lies became the accepted truth by them, and by everybody. The secret societies shouted longer and louder, manipulated harder and better than everyone else until their manufactured reality became the accepted one.

Now during the lifetimes of Lucy and Adrian, ninety-nine percent of earthbound humanity was in complete subservience to this false reality. Waking up from such a nightmare could not come without wrenching pain and suffering. In fact, these lies were now woven into the very genetic structure and psyche of earthbound humanity. Only a benevolently guided and willingly accepted genetic mutation within humanity initiated by the Celestial Fellowship could liberate earthbound humans from the malevolent shackles created by eons of manipulative deceptions and deprivations.

16. Initiation

"It's just a cow," Richard thought, "and a baby one at that." He was in college at his father's alma mater Ivy League school and was nearly through the initiation into the secret society his father belonged to and his grandfather had belonged to before him. Richard was being given the final test of sacrificing a cow. There he stood in an inner room with his body covered in a makeshift sheet and his head covered by a hood. In his right hand, he held a large, painstakingly sharp sacrificial knife.

Tied up in front of him was a very young, very panic-stricken Jersey heifer. Richard gazed into its gentle, large brown eyes. A faint memory of his joyful days of milking Phoebe on his mother's farm passed briefly through his mind. Shaking the memory away, he firmly held the heifer's head and pressed his knife hard against its throat. He took a breath and then slashed into her jugular vein as he had been instructed to do. The heifer's tethered legs kicked wildly for a few minutes as blood spurted out of her neck all over the floor, the sheet, his clothes beneath, and the alter. The sight sickened Richard for a moment but he steeled himself against it. He had to do what he had to do, after all. He vaguely saw her beautiful eyes glaze over and then her body sag against the ropes. Richard didn't really see this, though, because he was blocking the experience out almost as fast as it was happening. He turned and walked away still clutching the knife in his hand. He was now a full member of the Society.

And that is how it would be for him as a member with all of his future blood sacrifices. Unlike his fellow dark lords in training, he did not get recharged by the pain and suffering of others. Nor did he ever enter into a full demonic possessed state like his comrades did. For him, participating in these sacrifices took an act of will and was only done to show the others how tough he was and to prove that he belonged. But with each passing ritual, a part of Richard retreated and he withdrew more and more of his essence to a locked place deep inside himself.

Richard found that the deeper he went into the philosophy and mindset of his unholy guild, the more he was peeling the onion of a dark and self-destructive madness that held all of the members in its grip. But as disturbing as the philosophy of his secret group was, the ritualistic, sacrificial events it held were even more terrifying. These events had such a wild, almost otherworldly, quality to them. The beating drums, the moans and wails, and the bloodlust took him — took all of them — to a dark hypnotic place. Through these rituals, everyone in the group entered into an altered state of consciousness that can only be described as demonic. Sometimes Richard looked around at some of his cohorts who were otherwise known to be rich, refined young men and was troubled. Many of them he had known for years. He observed that every one of them got a very specific twisted expression on their faces during these sacrifices, with demonic eyes and sickening smiles that made them almost unrecognizable to him. He wondered if his face changed in the same way.

Death, blood, sex and destruction were generally the theme of these rituals in one way or another. It took some time for Richard to get used to the ever present coffins, bones, blood and shame. His fellow members scrupulously bowed before the demonic appropriators, shared their darkest secrets and pledged eternal loyalty and secrecy to them and to each other. However, what creeped Richard out the most was what happened back when he had just passed through his initiation.

Officially a sworn member by dint of full initiation, Richard was able to start getting a much clearer view of what the Society was, who was in it, and what their aims were. Adrian had given Richard hints over the years about all of this, of course, and had planted suggestions in his mind but even with that Richard had had no idea of the level of power and control these secret societies wielded throughout the world. He had had no idea from where this power and control came or how it came. Now that he was initiated, however, all of this was coming rapidly into view. Richard and the handful of other young men who had been initiated at the same time were being carefully indoctrinated into the full story. They learned that many years ago beings from another planet, powerful warriors and very technologically advanced, began visiting the Earth. Their visits became frequent enough and permanent enough that they directed the building of pyramids at many sites on the Earth which became a part of their interplanetary relay system. Through the development of religions and the shaping and retelling of human history, they had had a profound impact on subsequent human culture. One lasting way in which they forever changed human culture was by giving a select few humans the rites and technologies by which these humans could control the rest of humanity in their name.

Under the guidance of these extraterrestrial warriors, Richard's Society and other scattered secret groups across the Earth slowly gained control over the entire planet. They carried out the plans given to them nearly flawlessly through the mechanism of their compulsive and repetitive behaviors, thoughts and rituals. They were able to create their own paradigms, build nations, generate technological movements, control worldwide currencies and start wars all to solidify their grip on the world. The secret clubs and societies had no country of origin and their members moved from place to place when necessary in order to execute a new part of their plan. Now after millennia of using the geometrically increasing earthbound human population to extract vast resources from the Earth and from each other and for following directions for making major jumps in technological development, it was time to drastically reduce the Earth's population to a desirable level and implode the whole system in a controlled manner.

Richard was already aware that the Earth's human population had been growing largely unchecked for hundreds of years. What had never occurred to him before, though, was the possibility that this had been purposefully arranged. He never imagined that the planned outcome of the move towards modern methods of agriculture, industrial food production, modern medicine, education, and so on was to smooth out the natural ebbs and flows that used to keep humanity's population in balance. In so doing, they deliberately skewed the gene pool of earthbound humanity towards the weak, both physically and mentally. The weak were kept alive and reproducing at almost any cost. The result was that with each generation, modern human beings were born weaker and weaker. They were now so much weaker than humans used to be that they did not even remember the strength their forefathers had. They no longer knew that such strength and acuity as their ancestors had had was even possible.

However, the time of usefulness of this ever growing, ever weakening population to the dark appropriators was apparently at an end. It was made clear to Richard that his secret brethren wanted to reduce the Earth's population for selfish reasons. They were not at all concerned about what was good for humanity or the Earth they inhabited. They only knew that it was time to reduce numbers and that the "livestock" they saw all around them were too weak for them to take notice of anyway.

Richard also sensed that there was another reason behind this obsession with eugenics but no one he talked to knew what that was or even sensed as he did that there was another reason. He could not know that it was not in the Great Usurpers' interest to divulge to their under lords in the secret societies their own strategic reasons for population reduction. He did see, though, that his brothers in the Society thought that they knew everything. He wondered if they really did. It struck him occasionally that mostly they just did what they were ordered to do and that it took reaching out into the darkness and connecting with these powerful dark spirits to get them the power they needed to complete their work.

Richard and his cohort of new members were also thoroughly taught an array of symbols and numbers that were used as code and were planted everywhere for conveying hidden instructions. They were carefully schooled in the meanings and histories of these numbers and symbols. There was a lot to learn in this area and they spent quite a bit of time on it. They were shown how all of humanity was led to unknowingly bow before the symbols of the secret tribe's hidden deities which were placed on money, sculptures, architecture, music, advertising and media of all types. They were shown how even seemingly spontaneous events were actually planned to coincide with the patterns these numbers and symbols formed. Earthbound humans were quite unaware that they bowed before their ancient enemy who was working meticulously for their complete destruction but the Society members knew it and gloried in it.

The whole picture as he could now see it both disgusted and enthralled Richard. He was drawn to the potential of wielding so much power but was mortified at the cruelty that would be required for carrying out the plan as he understood it. His fellow members, on the other hand, often referred to the other people on the planet as if they were an inferior, domesticated species whose only purpose was to serve their illuminated brethren anyway so they expressed no compunction whatsoever about eliminating such dead weight from the surface of the earth in due course.

It took some time for Richard to digest all that was taught this even though he had grown up for most of his life with hints and suggestions along these lines from his father and others. Adrian had repeatedly mentioned to him during his school years that the history that was taught in schools and conveyed through the media was just propaganda to deceive the masses. In fact, he said, the entire cultural teaching fed to the masses was filled with lies and false so-called scientific principles. Adrian had told his son that these stories and illusions were fabricated and maintained to keep humanity from accessing their true potential and to keep them weak and dependent. Richard remembered that his father always had a glint in his eye when he said this.

However, even with this background from his childhood,

Richard had some difficulty in waking up now and accepting that everything that he had been told by the schools, the media and practically everyone else was a purposeful, complex lie. The people on Earth were under a massive delusion. One day they would all be forced to wake up with a violent jolt. He wondered what that would be like. Despite reassurances from his comrades that this phase would pose no real problem or threat, he had the sense that this would be a very scary prospect indeed.

After his great awakening, the academic year was over and Richard returned to his father's house for the summer. When Richard got home, his father was out of the country. About a week later, he returned and had breakfast the next morning with his son. Over toast and pleasantries, Adrian noticed his son as he had never noticed him before. The expression on his face changed and he steadily gazed at Richard with a look that seemed to say, "You know then?" Richard returned his gaze briefly but it was long enough to allow something to pass between them. Richard was one of them now, Adrian could see, and he beamed with the power of a person who was just about to conquer the world.

17. In the Weeds

One of the biggest obstacles facing the Celestial Fellowship in their task of helping earthbound humans liberate themselves from their Earthly prison was the very short lifespan of modern humans. Elsewhere in the galaxy most evolved beings lived several hundreds of earth years while many even lived lives thousands of years long. For those advanced souls, death as we know it did not exist. Rather at the end of their time, they only shifted to a more subtle form of life while still retaining their personal essence. Life moved much more slowly and naturally for these souls with little of the pressure or competing demands on their time that so many modern earthbound humans lived with.

In fact all higher developed beings were designed to live happy and restful lives although earthbound humans rarely had the opportunity to do so by this point. Plus they grew quickly and their phases of life were relatively compressed. Before they knew it they went from childhood to being parents and providers. The daily work required by their economic systems was constant and consumed many hours of each day. They had little meaningful contact with each other or with the earth that was designed to sustain them. Health issues galore often set in as they swiftly aged. Families did not stay together during the modern age so old age was often spent in isolation and pain. There were the occasional privileged few who got some time here or there to reflect and contemplate life. But even those few individuals had a very limited window during their lives for discovering their true inner nature as doing so was an effortful process for humans that generally required thousands of earth years and lives before reaching its culmination.

Most other evolved life forms had a much longer time period in their lives for growing into adulthood and their adult duties were not piled on top of each other within a few decades as was the case with earthbound humans. This compression of numerous duties and goals in human lives created debilitating exhaustion, bewilderment and sandwich generations of all kinds on Earth. Other evolved life forms were not forced to scramble for their daily bread for years on end. Their parenting phase was a long drawn-out process rooted in extensive community collaboration and time-tested systems for child rearing that were efficient, natural and congruent with their needs and goals. In fact, each phase of life had its appropriate focus which everyone knew and accepted. Nobody was rushed through a stage nor did anyone have to manage multiple phases of life work all at the same time and basically on their own.

Modern earthbound humans, on the other hand, were always in a frenzied rush comparatively speaking. They had to cope with overlapping developmental phases. In some cultures, at the peak of their economic or physical phase of productivity, they were also in the throes of parenting. This meant that they had to climb the highest hills of their life's material work at the same time that they were required to carefully guide the development of the future of their species. The additional creations of debt-based economies and frenzy-inducing technologies added exponentially to the madness. In short, modern earthbound humans were in a constant state of bombardment and distractible overwhelm.

There was a phrase used by the staff in some restaurants at the time to describe being busy and hopelessly behind to the point of utter collapse. It was "in the weeds." Being "in the weeds" meant that you were standing in weeds too thick to walk through. Some of those weeds were already tall, some were getting taller by the minute, while others were quickly sprouting all around you. Fast and thick the weeds were gaining ground. In restaurants, this translated into waiters with more tables than they could possibly serve and more customers waiting to be seated. Kitchen staff had more orders than they could fill with more pouring in. Tables were filling almost faster than they could be cleaned and set. Orders were coming in faster than they were going out. When, in the heat of the moment, a few mistakes were made resulting in orders having to be corrected or redone, real chaos set in. Rectifying these mistakes took time and attention that the server or cook didn't have available. They could not keep all of their immediate tasks within their conscious minds so there would be a growing sense of spiraling out of control.

The restaurant would get busier and busier and the weeds kept growing up around the staff. The pace became frenetic. The stress level would rise until the service ended and the restaurant emptied out. By the end of the shift, the staff members would be completely exhausted by the sheer energy they had just put out and by the output of adrenalin it had taken for them to complete their work. There would be no energy left to reflect or evolve. Rather, staff members would simply wind down the best that they could, go to sleep, wake up, and do the whole thing all over again their next shift.

As a rule, earthbound humans were living their entire lives very much in the weeds during these modern days. Day in and day out, they were dogged by a mad race just to survive. Actual thriving was completely out of the question. This reality represented a large problem for the Celestial Fellowship. Where were the earthbound humans going to get the time to go within and find their true inner natures? This was especially challenging as very few of those humans even knew that doing so was a possibility in the first place. Of those who did, few as yet had any conscious desire to do so ina systematic or thorough way.

This problem was obviously going to get worse and not better as soon as the many upheavals that the Earth was about to experience destabilized the planet. People would have to work twice as hard just to eke out the most meager of livings. Contemplation and inner research would be out of the question. So it was going to take a great deal of work and ingenuity from the Celestial Fellowship to slow everything down and help the earthbound humans internalize themselves now while there was a little time.

108

One idea that came out of several of the projection models the Celestial Fellowship generated on the subject indicated that the restoration of the family was a necessity for helping people slow down and reflect. To be exact, it seemed that a loving family environment functioning within a supportive agrarian village or tribal situation was essential to general human evolution. In order to discover their true inner nature, earthbound humans needed to be encouraged to live in cooperative, family-based agrarian villages with enough supportive technology, knowledge and resources available to get their collective needs met, both physically and spiritually.

In fact one of the evil strategies that had been gradually implemented over the last couple of hundred years by the Great Usurpers and their earthbound dark planners was to unravel agrarian life as well as destroy the family unit as a means for gaining total control over their subjects. With the Great Usurpers having studied humans as closely as they had, they knew that doing these two things would shift the masses away from their inherent dependence upon nature and each other and forcibly into depending upon their dark system instead. This would go very far in making people weak, vulnerable and compliant.

Through their dark planners, the Great Usurpers designed systems in which individuality was emphasized to the detriment of the centuries' old traditional emphasis on family, tribe, community. This calculated redirection of energy eventually led to earthbound humans adopting a star mentality. Everybody wanted to be the center of attention all of the time. They all wanted to be kings and divas and CEO's and stars. There were very few humans left who were willing to be supportive role players and make it possible for a family or a community to maintain its health and continuity. Especially targeted for this were women. It was women, in particular, who had to be pulled away from their natural inclination to support others and serve their families and communities for this dramatic shift to take place. Luring them into the marketplace was an important step towards making them vulnerable to the notion of competing to be stars themselves. Their withdrawal from their families and communities in turn left family and community members more vulnerable to falling into the star mentality as well.

The dark planners' system stressed attitudes of selfishness and entitlement. Earthbound humans became un-teachable and unwilling to accept truths that conflicted with their personal views of how the world should be. Personal views more often than not placed the narcissistic individual at the center of the universe. As a result of such attitudes and mental and emotional habits, earthbound humans got so that they had trouble even being in a family or community. Family members or community members working harmoniously together to fulfill group needs was no longer a natural Earthly occurrence. Instead fractured families and what was left of any kind of communities spent most of their time and energy intensely negotiating each person's role along with each person's rewards or privileges. These long, dragged out negotiations and re-negotiations sabotaged any chance of people actually working together cooperatively during the short period of time they had together on the planet.

The most powerful tool the Great Usurpers created to force this profound shift in earthbound humans away from their natural cooperative ways and towards these competitive, selfish ways was their system of monetary rewards. They arranged for people to become conditioned to expect a reward for doing any work at all. Even modern day children expected monetary rewards for contributing to their very own family. This "what's in it for me" attitude became the rule of the day. In fact, the almighty American dollar covered with Great Usurper symbology became an idol worshipped by many around the world. It came to be that no human could live in the world without having to bow down and worship this demonic note with its evil eye radiating out of the capstone, watching and controlling all. People no longer prayed for love, or for heightened abilities, or for needs to get met, or for the strength to do their work. Instead they prayed for money, money and more money and all of the power they thought it would give them.

With the advent of humans worshipping money came also the advent of them giving up their innate abilities. To the increasingly limited human mind, money was like God in many ways. God is nothing or nothingness in a way but from God all is possible. God is potential. Money is also nothing. Money has literally no value in and of itself. It is a piece of paper that represents potential. In a sense, God and money seem alike in that they only become something if an evolved being takes the idea of them and uses their creative force to manifest it into something.

The trick that the Great Usurpers and their dark planning human cohorts played on the earthbound humans was getting them to believe that they could not do anything, receive anything or become anything without money. Society became the ultimate pyramid scheme. The dark ones even displayed their pyramid right on the American dollar. The appropriators and the dark planners successfully convinced the people of Earth that they needed money to manifest their ideas into reality. Money became the only source of energy that counted or was thought to be real.

In truth, earthbound humans were designed with everything already within them necessary for creating whatever they needed to sustain their material existence. They had the ultimate potential of God in their hearts - the medium for all creation. They had a mind that could generate ideas and that connected with the ideas and acted on them. They had receptive minds that could be inspired with the specific ideas that they needed. They had an almost limitless creative force, as well as the will force and the physical body necessary for doing the work involved in manifesting their ideas. They gravitated towards living in very useful social systems (families, tribes, villages) which supported humans in manifesting together what their needs required. They were also connected with an enduring support system of spiritual beings and extraterrestrial well wishers who were always available for guidance and support, whether or not the humans were actually conscious of them.

With so many gifts, the earthbound human did not need money as a middle man to make real life possible. In fact, money was an impediment to their real life as the dark planners used money and the whole money system to extract a tax on human potential. Now that people had been duped into believing that they could not survive without it, the money system was being used as a weapon to mire earthbound humans down in crushing debt. This rendered them permanent slaves to the system. People had been reduced to spending all of their adult lives in a frenzied rat race of trying to work their way out of their debt-based prison. Their real potential was being siphoned off by the dark planners' unnatural monetary system.

The rat race, as the earthbound humans themselves had come to refer to their daily lives, was purposely set up by the Great Usurpers with the idea that it would deprive modern humans of the time, tolerance or patience it took to have a meaningful family life and to conscientiously and lovingly undertake the hard work that goes into conducting family life. This rat race carried earthbound humans so far away from their original model of life that money came to displace the family in their hearts and lives. Earthbound humans were led to the astonishing conclusion that they no longer needed to depend on God, themselves or even their families in order to thrive in the world. Faith in these powerful natural systems was overthrown and people became totally dependent upon money.

Family was the human's natural support system. Cows lived in herds, birds in flocks, fish in schools and lions in prides. People lived in families. This was an important consideration when attempting to shape human behavior. If one person in a family were to wake up out of the dream of the debt-based, pyramidal monetary scheme that sucked the very marrow out of a human life, that person would be pretty helpless to create radical change in their lives until other members of their family also woke up out of that dream. Working together they would have a chance, at least, of significantly changing their way of thinking and their way of life.

For the Celestial Fellowship's effort at ennobling the earthbound human to be successful, then, earthbound people had to be restored back into family life. People would have to choose to relearn how to slow down, how to be together, how to see life through new eyes. They would have to change their goals and orientation towards life. They would have to become agreeable to contributing to their families and communities without thought of personal reward, fame or fortune. A natural life lived together would have to become the reward. Being able to contribute work and service towards a better life would have to become the prize. Once the demonic monetary system collapsed, people would no longer be in a position to consider themselves as individuals who didn't need anything else or anyone else in order to be successful. Instead they would be led back to finding fulfillment in doing their duty and contributing whatever they had to offer simply because that was what they were born to do.

From their observations, the Celestial Fellowship could see that the restoration of the earthbound human family could give rise to a great awakening and a profound strengthening of the race. They had hope that the impending destruction and resulting harsh living conditions of the future that the humans were going to have to endure would work to the highest and bring the human family back together again. If this were achieved, then earthbound humans would have a fighting chance at rediscovering their divine inner nature.

18. Obelisks and Radiant Hearts

At this point in his young adult life, Richard found himself wandering around lost in the world with nothing to believe in and nothing to value. Power did not have as much appeal for him as it did for the other members of his secret guild. Wielding power did feel familiar to him, though. He felt as if he had been down this road before, the road of power and control, but he also had the vague feeling that it hadn't ended well. This faint inner resistance to indulgence in power and gluttony zapped any emotional reward that he might have gotten from such pursuits. So Richard's interest in power and control in this life faded fairly quickly. He had the sense that the oppressive power that was extracted from abuse and domination was short lived and shallow anyway.

Deep down, he knew that the quest for complete earthly domination would backfire in the end. All historical campaigns to conquer the world had ended in failure. Richard had no reason to believe that this one would be any different. He witnessed how sloppy and incompetent many of the comrades in his secret guild were which did not inspire confidence in the overall success of their quest. He played along like he was invested in his group as he had nowhere else to go. And, frankly, he was curious to see how their schemes would play out. Life for him was more or less a spectator sport at this point. He felt dead inside. He did not have a goal or anything to believe in so he watched and waited.

There were times when his conscience got the better of him however. His father had not been successful in completely destroying the positive character qualities that Lucy had instilled in her son during those first seven years together. There was still some softness in him, some compassion for others. Part of him was appalled by the plans of his powerful guild members to bring humanity to its knees. He toyed with the idea of exposing the secret societies but who would he tell? His group ran the media, the government, the law enforcement agencies and everything else that mattered. The masses clearly did not want to know about how the world really worked and who ran it anyway. They were generally content to indulge in their own pleasures and addictions as they were being blindly led to their slaughter.

The secret societies' machinations could hardly be called true secrets anyway. For years the dark planners had been slowly and subtly releasing their plans to the media in order to accustom the masses to the dismantling of their civil liberties. It is an unwritten rule that all highly evolved beings must make their plans and intentions publicly known before those plans and intentions can come to fruition. Good beings, for the most part, can keep their plans open anyway as they have nothing to hide. That is, unless they live in an abusive, violent world in which their positive plans could result in imprisonment or death. However even in the face of danger or ridicule, they still have to open their goals up to the universe in some way in order to let in the power or creative force required for manifesting those goals. A seed can germinate in darkness, but when it sprouts it needs to present itself to the sunlight in order to grow into what it is meant to become.

This same rule of having to share goals in some way applied just as stringently to the dark planners but since they lived on the wrong side of the law, they essentially had to steal the creative force needed to manifest their goals. Good people who are following natural law and receiving information from above can attract creative force and experience the universe blessing and supporting their work. The dark planners whose plans went against natural law, however, could only steal creative energy from humans in order to make their abominations a reality. To do this, they introduced their schemes to earthbound humans as the opposite of what they really were and disguised them with lots of pomp and circumstance. This almost always resulted in sufficiently deceiving the masses that they signed off on whatever the nasty scheme was. For example, if a secret guild wanted to poison the masses in a particular way, they sold the poison as medicine. If they planned to enslave the masses in a particular way, they sold that form of slavery as freedom.

No matter which scheme they were pushing, they had to sell it with a lot of hype, and manipulative and subliminal sales techniques designed to create enthusiasm and a buzz within the population. It always worked. People eagerly lined up to get the ball rolling. They start making the scheme a reality themselves. In this way, the dark planners who lacked their own access to the creative force twisted and bent the creative energy of their subjects into that which would fulfill the will of their slave masters. Since the Great Usurpers' plans for complete dominion over the earth were in the quickening phase, the dark planners instinctively stepped up the pace of releasing bits and pieces of information about their nefarious schemes out to the public.

The masses could not see the plans for what they were. They never could see them for what they were because the masses basically refused to believe that such dark actions could be taken by their leaders or by any humans at all. This was in spite of all of the evidence that was right before their eyes. Instead their minds succumbed to the deceptive spin and the addictive advertising that made these schemes sound righteous and beneficial for all. Eventually the masses always signed off on the scams in one way or another. By now, even if the secret societies told people pointblank about their plots and their real attitude about humanity, very few earthbound humans would take their confessions seriously. Most were so frozen in their beliefs that they couldn't even glimpse how desperate their situation was. They could not imagine the possibilities or acknowledge the horror that was about to befall them. It just couldn't be and so, as far as they were concerned, it wasn't.

No, there was no out for Richard. He was simply going to have to go along for the ride and see where it took him. This became very obvious to him when he first stumbled on the long history of using obelisks to control the masses. He stumbled on the information that obelisks were first put to use by the Great Usurpers way back when they started enslaving humanity thousands of years ago. The obelisks were used to transmit low frequency vibrations that blocked their slaves' ability to find God within themselves. The overlords had ordered their human slaves to build obelisks by the score ages ago in order to establish their own agenda from the start.

Drawing on this ancient technology, Richards's secret society members had had some of the ancient obelisks transported to North America as well as had new ones constructed and planted in every major city that they controlled. They did this for the same reason that the Usurpers had built them so many years ago – to keep humanity on its knees. Richard became kind of obsessed with these obelisks even to the extent of visiting most of the ones around the country during his odd bits of free time from college. Ironically a number of them were revered as national and historical landmarks. To his surprise, Richard found that he was sensitive to the hostile, low level vibratory frequencies these demonic pillars emitted. He could feel them weakening him whenever he stood near them. Their vibrations insinuated their way into him and left trails and pockets of dullness and befuddlement behind them.

Whenever he visited an obelisk, Richard looked around the busy area where it was located and observed how oblivious the many people around it were to the vibrational poison that was keeping them in shackles. He watched the people as they took photos and ogled and celebrated these demonic totem poles that were deadening them a little more each day. At each obelisk, he served as a witness. He cringed at the sight of innumerable people bowing down before the idols that enslaved them. After observing this countless times, any hope that he still had was extinguished. He decided that there was nothing for him to do but just go enjoy himself the best he could in the time remaining. Any resistance to this vast, mad plan was clearly futile. The people of Earth, his human brothers and sisters, were gorging themselves on the very poisons that were robbing them of their humanity.

What Richard did not know was that all of this time the Divine Hierarchy of the Celestial Fellowship had been transmitting their own vibrations and moving their own plans forward as well. Many evolved earthbound human souls were in contact with these benevolent beings whether they knew it consciously or not. They received divine grace from the Entrusted Ones and often unknowingly passed it along to their earthbound brothers and sisters. The hearts of those who were willing to open themselves up to the natural universe were being refined by the Celestial Fellowship. Gradually their hearts were becoming conduits for the subtle, God-infused vibrations that were being directed towards the Earth in order to divinize it.

Living anonymously across the globe, these pure souls operating under the instruction and guidance of an evolved Spiritual Master transmitted these most pure and subtle vibrations through their hearts. As instructed, they spent their leisure hours cleaning the atmosphere around them and filling it with divine love.

Richard was totally unaware that such a network existed and that his mother was a part of it. If he had known this, his eventual choice would have been made easier. He would have been able to see that the apparent invincibility of the all-powerful dark forces that ruled the planet was a sham. He would have understood that his pedigreed secret society was just a bunch of naughty boys who had gained power temporarily and through ignominious means. Furthermore, they had gained this power only because they were backed by a very limited extra-terrestrial species that was about to make what would probably be a failed attempt at usurping the will of God. These societies also had some limited backing from the Celestial Fellowship as well because the dark planners were willing to do the much needed work of destroying the modern day system which was a necessary step before a spiritual renaissance could take place on Earth.

So the image of inevitable success which the Great Usurpers and their earthly dark lords were so adroitly able to convey was just an illusion. Soon a very different sort of reality was going to hit home.

19. Planes of Existence

At one time or another, most modern earthbound humans had had the uneasy feeling that something terribly significant was missing from their lives. They felt an indescribable loneliness accompanied by an acute sense that something just wasn't right. This experience was often particularly painful when a person was facing a problem or a situation that felt too big or too difficult for them to handle. Try as they might, they found that they were just not equipped to deal with the issue effectively. It was almost as if the skill required for coping with the problem, or the ability or insight or other inner resource necessary for resolving the problem which should have been built into their system from the beginning was missing. There was a vague feeling that they should have been able to connect with something "inner" or "higher" that would have helped them navigate through their troubled time but yet nothing inside or outside of them seemed to come to their aid. So they floundered endlessly in a dull sea of difficulty.

The fact of the matter was earthbound humans had had those inner resources built into their systems originally. In fact, traces of those inner resources still existed within them. They didn't know it and so had no idea how to access them. As luck would have it, both the Great Usurpers and the Celestial Fellowship had taken steps over the many years to block or at least limit human access to those inner resources, albeit for very different reasons. The Great Usurpers blocked their access in order to cloak their own agenda. The Celestial Fellowship blocked their access because of earthbound humans' destructive and aggressive tendencies. The result was the same, however. Earthbound humans struggled along on the physical plane because they didn't have access to any of the other planes of existence that would have illuminated their earthly experience and helped them navigate through troubled waters.

The larger truth was that human beings came equipped

with a physical body but they also came equipped with several related subtle bodies that have no physical properties or characteristics whatsoever, such as the mental body, the astral body, the causal body and so on. It was by use of these subtle bodies that humans were meant to reach into the past or the future, to reach into what is inner or higher, and to reach for new ideas and solutions. After ages of having their knowledge of these subtle bodies blocked, however, earthbound humans had become very solid creatures. Their scheming leaders and the leaders of those leaders had put a great deal of time and energy into blocking their access to these other parts of themselves. Due to this lack of connection, earthbound humans faced enormous obstacles when attempting to fully solve the challenges they faced. For one thing, they could usually only address the part of the problem that existed in their physical world. As the roots of their problems were not usually found in the physical world but on more subtle planes and as those subtle planes themselves had to be addressed and adjusted in order to fully resolve most problems, modern earthbound humans went through their lives bewildered and essentially crippled.

By blocking earthbound humanity's access to the more subtle planes of existence or consciousness, the Great Usurpers created a very advantageous working situation for themselves. They could operate on Earth cloaked in darkness as their actions and communications were completely invisible to the earthbound humans. Even better, from behind their shield of darkness they could plant suggestions in the humans' minds. With this technology of suggestion they could shape human behavior and feelings, guide social trends, and dictate technological and economic developments from within – or so it would seem to the humans.

Everything created by more highly developed beings started first as a thought which did its work on levels of existence that were subtler than the grosser world of physical things and actions. Human beings had thoughts and ideas come to them from this dimension of thought all of the time. However, they had been trained into the conveniently erroneous belief that this process of thinking and finding inspiration was a mental activity limited to their own brains, originating within their own brains. They were not aware that all of this took place on a plane of existence that was similar to one of their internet chat rooms. Most of their ideas actually came from mental and heart based flows of thought originating in a realm where beings of all types came together and shared and influenced each other.

Unfortunately for earthbound humans, they were largely unaware that they were in a chat room. On the subtle planes of existence, conversing or chatting was more like communing or sharing. There was a coming together in a faint and subtle way and information and feelings were exchanged. Earthbound humans were souls trapped in bodies that lived in a gross physical world full of sensory simulation, however. They had become accustomed to loud and forceful interactions and communications. This subtle body sharing of light and faint whispering interactions did not get their attention. Therefore, they had no idea that they were communing or with whom they were communing.

A rare few of them had the inner development to connect with higher members of their own kind, or with higher benevolent souls who perhaps existed in physical form on other planets, or with beings of energetic spirit who existed on other dimensions entirely. Most earthbound humans, though, were constantly receiving ideas from the Great Usurpers and their dark lords. Through this channel into human minds, the Great Usurpers had shaped great earthly movements in a direction favorable to their own ultimate designs.

At the same time that the Great Usurpers were affecting human life from another dimension, they seeded earthbound humanity with a deep suspicion of anything that smacked of contacts emanating from those other dimensions. They embedded into major religions the idea that such contacts were evil and from the devil. They also eventually encouraged the development of professional psychology which called such experiences of other realms symptoms of mental illness. By creating an ethic of shaming, ridiculing and ostracizing people who were able to connect with the spirit world, the dark planners effectively shut this avenue of possible support and information down for all of humanity.

The fact that earthbound humans were blocked from contact with the Celestial Heaven made it difficult for the Celestial Fellowship to do its work. The benevolent brotherhood wanted humans to know that they were being contacted and by whom. They needed earthbound humans to take responsibility and participate in these contacts as partners. Members of the Celestial Fellowship had nothing to hide and so did not benefit from the centuries of darkness, stealth and ignorance instituted by the Great Usurpers. While there needed to be a vibrational shield held up against the aggression and power-grabbing ignorance of humans who were existing on a dense vibrational plane, the Celestial Fellowship still wanted the people of Earth to know that they were all connected and that life is best lived by following the divine suggestions given to all of us through a subtle, inner connection with the Source.

Although a human's freedom to choose exists moment to moment, in reality there is ultimately only one choice and that is to follow those wise suggestions. Any being can refuse to make that choice for a time, even for multiple existences, but the choice to cooperate with our benevolent advisors will continually present itself until the chooser finally agrees to follow the true path. In reality, these apparent choices are really only a choice of whether or not to accept what is being given with love right now or delay the inevitable by wandering off on one's own idiosyncratic route first before painfully returning to what was so lovingly offered in the first place.

Deep inside, earthbound humans sensed what to do. They just had to act on it in order to experience the proof of the magnificence of what they sensed. If they could only agree to embrace the universal rules that bound all of life together, an abiding inner craving to connect with the Creator would flower and be fully, pervasively, compellingly felt. The intensity of this longing would lead them to turning within and to gradually internalizing their lives in all respects. In due course, these beings would naturally become more responsible and self-disciplined, more tolerant and loving, more flexible and open. Once humanity could manage to fully integrate this evolutionary step of internalizing their existence, greater levels of consciousness and vast subtle planes of existence would become open to them.

The battle on Earth, then, was really between those who were assisting human beings to evolve versus those who were blocking them from their natural evolution.

20. The Invisible Battle

It was hard to fully comprehend or even calculate the many genetic outcomes possible in the smorgasbord of DNA that made up the modern day earthbound human. Members of the elite secret societies of dark planners, for instance, had a great deal of Great Usurper DNA in their code. They were generally aware of this and purposefully intermarried with the goal of keeping their genetic line strong. After generations of careful interbreeding aimed at building a broad base from which to maintain intensely negative power and societal control, however, these humans eventually became prone to madness, deviant behaviors, self-hatred and other destructive tendencies. Meanwhile they had also worked to inject their genetic material into other population groups so that they could spread the influence of their line throughout society. In so doing, they had passed on many of their qualities to much of humanity and had also increased general human receptivity to the Usurpers' influence. Adrian's clan had an unusually large proportion of Great Usurper DNA in its genetic makeup. Family members of his clan tended to be inordinately proud of this fact.

Lucy's family, on the other hand, carried a preponderance of Pleiadian genetics as well as genetics from the highest group of extraterrestrials that had participated in the ongoing genetic experimentation on earthlings. Humans with these Celestial Fellowship based genetics were often not even aware of it. When they did become aware of it, their awareness was subtle and not really a concrete thought or fact. The idea might come to them from time to time that they were connected to and a part of something that was beyond human. From that realization they might feel compelled to help lift up the people around them and evolve more themselves. By becoming personally ennobled, they invariably raised up the human race as well. Often people with these genetics had the privilege of incarnating together. This was the case with Lucy and her family. They happily shared some of the higher characteristics and qualities available to earthbound humans. This added to the intimacy and joy they had shared together.

Within this uncontrolled mix of genetic material and spiritual intentions coming out of a combination of native Earth aboriginal, Great Usurper, Pleiadian and a number of other extraterrestrial genetics, there was yet another mixing which factored into the earthbound creature known as Richard Neil. Lucy and Adrian's son was genetically encoded by and open to both sides. He was sensitive to their respective approaches to work in their divergent realms of consciousness. Both Lucy and Adrian worked consciously and unconsciously on many planes of existence all of the time. Their work affected the world as a whole but much of it was directed more specifically at their son, Richard Neil.

Lucy worked primarily from her heart with love being the essential gift that she gave to her son. Love emanates from the subtle essence of our universe. Its effects surpass by far those of any other vibration. All beings come from love and every creature seeks contact with its loving Creator. It was with this subtlest medium that Lucy worked.

We are all compelled to find our way back to our original home. Richard was no different. As a young boy, he had basked in his mother's love and was completely content in that existence. Deep down, he had longed for pure love and craved finding his way back to his eternal home. Even as lost as he was now in his young adult years, the love his mother had transmitted to him during his early years still nurtured his heart. Her great love for him, and for the Divine, had planted the seeds in his heart for a future grand awakening that could take place when the conditions were right for her son to bloom.

Adrian and his crew countered others' use of love with fear, temptation and the hypnotic lure of power. Just as all beings have a craving to return to their original or divine home, they also have a curiosity about the dark side and a weakness for power. On the material level, Adrian used the temptations of the degraded and debauched world to lure his son into the darkness. However, Adrian worked on other planes of existence as well.

Just as the obelisks in public spaces radiated lower frequency vibrations in order to bring out the lower sides of humanity, Adrian filled his private home with objects, idols, thoughts and intentions that all emanated low frequency vibrations. He used his dark thoughts and intentions to saturate his son with the heavy and gross cosmic matter that would ultimately lead to his being lured into the world of darkness. Adrian also used his thought force to create an illusion wherein all the dark and fearful nightmares of this modern, material world were inextricably associated with God and religion.

His secret crew and the malevolent Usurpers had worked for years on infiltrating religious hierarchies and spiritual movements. Once they had gained sufficient influence and control within these hierarchies, they were able to wield supposedly religious authority for instituting their dark and evil acts in the name of God. From this they cultivated in earthbound humans the dark idea that God himself was responsible for this evil. The dark ones have always found ways to convince the masses that they were speaking and acting on God's behalf. This claiming of Divine will and energy was foundational to the Usurper movement. Adrian expanded upon this illusion by filling Richard's mind with the idea that God was behind all of the dark work that their secret guild was carrying out. He persuaded Richard to believe that God won by using force so, therefore, the use of force was Godly work. By means of such logic, Adrian turned Richard's unconscious craving to connect with God into a temptation for power and control.

Of course, Lucy and her group also used their thought force in specific ways to effect change. They had the benefit of being permitted to draw upon creative powers and divine inspiration and these they used artistically and sensitively within the thought realm to paint pictures in earthbound humans' minds of the beauty and perfection at the heart of the universe.

Lucy had another very powerful method of working as well. She prayed for her son fervently and continuously. When prayer for someone is rendered sincerely with love and purity, it is the most effective method for returning a soul to its natural condition and back towards its destiny. When someone is continuously prayed for by a refined and spiritually developed person, the person being prayed for is thereby placed in direct contact with the Divine Essence. This automatically brings that soul back into balance over the course of time. Once this process is activated, it can go on and on in ways both seen and unseen. Such prayer activates energies that slowly begin to move. The divine mechanism that awakens a soul and brings it to the feet of its Creator moves the initiate step by step through the layers of subtle existence to the Center of all that is.

This is why Adrian was not able to keep his son fully embedded in the dark side. Lucy's heartfelt prayers brought her son back to the divine over and over again and kept the natural forces constantly at work in bringing him back into balance. Events and experiences appeared naturally in Richards's life at critical moments that served to pull him away from the extreme darkness at the periphery of the universe where his father resided and back towards the center. This was exactly why the dark side could not afford to have earthbound humanity connecting with natural forces. Those forces might activate the innate balancing mechanisms that exist in all being and foil their plans.

In addition to prayer, Lucy and the great advisors used the power of suggestion for creating positive change. Sometimes the love that Lucy transmitted to her son contained within it the merest, and yet most potent, subtle suggestions. These suggestions worked like a tonic on all levels of his being and for his good. Her subtle thoughts created the potential in her son for the development of the character qualities he would need for his work as a great redeemer of humanity. Lucy's suggestions also reinforced her son's inner fortitude which he needed for

128

battling the demons his father was constantly surrounding him with. Lucy could even use her love and thought force to go back in time and plant suggestions within her son's past experiences, both in this life and in past lives, that would start those qualities developing, on a soul level, years prior in what was now considered to be the past.

Adrian and his side countered such moves with intense work on the subconscious level of Richard's mind. The dark planners had long understood that in each person's subconscious mind there lurked an array of powerful archetypes ranging from good to bad, from constructive to destructive They had long understood that within the earthbound human's subconscious mind existed all of the horrors and demonic creations that the Great Usurpers and their dark planners had created and embellished over the millennia. They had long taken advantage of the fact that within the earthbound human's subconscious mind existed all of the predatory creatures, both imagined and real, that have lived on in nightmarish myths and legends, frightening people in horror stories, dreams and rituals throughout their troubled history on this planet.

In order to direct this subconscious energy, the dark planners commandeered the complex system of symbology used on Earth since ancient times. They had warped those symbols to their own ends so that they would arouse specific negative archetypes in people and unleash enormous uncontrolled energy. The dark planners had also invented clever ways of insinuating their symbols into peoples' minds until by Richard's time these symbols literally saturated the environment of the modern human being. Every day people were exposed to symbols of weapons, snakes, pyramids, goats, a devilish owl, twin pillars, and an all-seeing eye among many others. In this way, the secret societies and the Usurping overlords drove deep into the human subconscious the idea that darkness is all powerful and its victory inevitable. With these symbols, the dark planners claimed the planet and marked it just as a predatory animal marks its territory with urine.

To tailor this overwhelming symbolic display of power and control specifically to Richard, Adrian meticulously surrounded Richard with as many subliminal suggestions as were available to him to make sure that his son believed completely that darkness held all the power and that his only choice was to join his demonic brethren in their quest for dominion. Everywhere Richard looked in the world controlled by his father, he saw the symbolic display of the power and control over the world wielded by his father's secret guild. There was nowhere that he could gaze and not see the mark of the beast claiming ownership of all that existed.

Over and over again Lucy and her benevolent advisors healed her son of the ongoing subconscious assault by repairing the perforations in his astral body and by cleaning the spiritual refuse that accumulated on his other subtle spiritual bodies. One thing the Great Usurpers and their earthbound minions had never been able to completely control was a human being's ability to travel to different planes of existence through meditation, prayer and dreams or a human's ability to draw to themselves guardian angels and spirits of one sort or another. So during the peaceful hours of the night, Richard's subtle bodies found their way to the nourishing places in the universe where repairs could be made and cleaning could be done and benevolent souls could surround him, giving him balance, perspective and healing.

Even the benevolent energetic beings and the negative entities that were linked to Richard fought battles of higher and lower vibrations and attitudes, each influencing Richard with their essence and intentions. No stone was left unturned and every level of consciousness or plane of existence was activated and used to either support or destroy Richard's connection with the Divine.

In all of this back and forth, each side had its own ways of appealing to Richard. On the one hand by appealing to Richard's senses, addictions, animal instincts, fears, desires and past

130

mistakes, Adrian relentlessly drew his son toward the all-consuming darkness. On the other hand, Lucy appealed to Richard's innate longing to be connected to his internal Beloved. As with all humans, this longing was fueled by the deep, pervasive, inner pain that inspires beings to throw off their superficial individuality and merge with the divine essence that resides in their hearts.

All of these forms of input, and tugs back and forth, and woundings and healings, and comings and goings blended together to make up the background behind Richard's ultimate future choice between his mother's ways or his father's. On top of his already tumultuous life on an unstable planet, Richard's energetic components were being pulled back and forth like a yo-yo between these two competing sides. When Richard was with his mother during his early years and during his visits with her and the year he spent with her on her farm, he was not only experiencing different physical conditions but his subtle bodies were also being enhanced by the positive forces that existed in and around his mother. While at his father's home and in his company, Richard's subconscious mind was being meddled with constantly. Day in and day out his father was beating the drum that pounded in the subliminal messages of his dark choosing.

To make matters worse, the conditions of life on Earth generally inhibited a human from making much conscious contact with either of these more subtle sides of themselves or the planes of existence on which these sides operated. Therefore earthbound humans were blind to the ropes that tugged and pulled them around like rag dolls.

Earth had long been a major battleground between good and evil. Both the positive and negative forces in the universe had staked out territory around and inside this small planet third from its sun millennia ago. These forces were embedded in and surrounded everything on this planet. There were spirits, atoms, molecules, sprites, jinn, angels, demons and every imaginable being and subtle force operating on various planes of existence doing their work to inspire or coerce humanity to their given side.

During all of Richard's life, the dark side of this battle had had the advantage. The dark planners, the members of Richards's secret guild, had worked for hundreds of years to publicly ridicule and dismiss the belief in other planes of existence. They had created cultures in which most of the people mocked and laughed at those who believed in and communicated with inter-dimensional beings of any type. So while earthbound humans experienced nothing but isolation, the dark planners enjoyed full contact with their inter-dimensional and extraterrestrial support team which controlled and supported them in every aspect of their work.

So these dark planners had put themselves in a winning position. They controlled most of the world's resources and directed economic systems at will. They owned the media and shaped to their own ends the historical narrative, education and technology. They had access to large armies and to information that the rest of the people on the Earth did not have access to. In fact most of the rest of the people on Earth had nothing but faulty information and broken systems with which to navigate their lives.

The dark planners also had another advantage. They had the advantage of force. Their negative support team, led by the Great Usurpers, was prone to using force and heavy handed tactics of all kinds. Their influence and agenda was always thrust upon humanity. The Celestial Fellowship, on the other hand, was much gentler in their approach to guiding humanity to a righteous path. They gave only subtle invitations and support to the earthbound humans. To receive this support, the earthbound humans had to actively choose to connect to their benevolent support team. If they did not manage to reach up and accept the Celestial Fellowship's generous and loving offer for being raised to a higher level of consciousness, they would instead be indoctrinated and controlled by the dark side by default. A non-choice inevitably led to an uncontested victory by the dark side.

With so many stumbling blocks in the way, only a rare

few earthbound humans were acquainted with even the most rudimentary aspects of the spiritual science of connecting with the Celestial Fellowship. Few knew of the practices and attitudes that would make connection possible. Some realized that when a human being is in distress and beseeches God in a humble and prayerful mood, this opens the door for the human soul and the body it inhabits to be surrounded by loving and supportive beings. They knew that this could bring a feeling of being embraced and enhanced, of being in the flow of life. Some people experienced being lifted up and ennobled. They became capable of resonating with a higher vibrational level and, therefore, lived their lives differently. They began to long to be divinized.

There were a very few who knew that when a human being lives a disciplined life of restraint and moderation and when they eat healthy foods and live simple and natural lives, they would more easily be able to access the higher planes of existence. They would be able to tune into divine beings and channel their wisdom and suggestions. Human life could become a hymn of love to the Divine. This was why Richard did so well living with his mother. While with her, he lived a natural life and the beings surrounding him were part of the Celestial Fellowship. They had lifted him upwards.

However when he was with his father, Richard was surrounded by darkness and gross foods and activities and people of all types. The heaviness weighed on him. His deteriorating mental and spiritual condition led to poor choices in thought and deed which created avenues for the dark forces of the universe to overwhelm him through the forceful occupation of his person. Demons have long fed on the negative emotions arising from the overall gross condition of the human experience on earth. They have attached themselves to people and incited them to rage, fear, torture, and abuse. Demons have manipulated the choices of men towards perpetual war, famine, injustice and overall suffering so that they could feast on the anguish of the moaning masses.

So with all of these forces in play, Richards's ultimate choice of side would be momentous in terms of its importance. Given the intensity of input from both sides into his system, the complex nature of even an ordinary life on Earth at this time, and the bumps and bruises from his own tumultuous past life history on this planet, it would be a wonder if Richard did not go mad before he ever got around to making his choice. So how would he make his epic choice between these two vast, ancient, polarized forces?

21. Humanity is Being Groomed

In spite of the tug of war being waged in his mind, Richard still managed to retain a high degree of curiosity about the world around him. In fact, one of his saving graces turned out to be that he thoroughly enjoyed watching "the game," as he liked to call it. Richard had always been interested in social dynamics and was particularly fascinated by how people oriented themselves to the world. He had always watched people closely. On his mother's farm he had even gotten a kick out of watching the chickens for hours on end and trying to figure out their language and their complex social system. He wondered how each role was chosen for each chicken in the flock. He puzzled over how when a chicken died or new hens or roosters were added to the flock, it sent a ripple effect through the whole social structure. He even noticed that events in chicken society played out in cyclical patterns. He wondered how that was possible and looked for similarities in human society. This habit of observing dynamics and patterns was like a mental hobby for Richard. It occupied him and gave him many useful insights.

So when Richard was initially given access to the myriad plans for manipulation, force and coercion that his secret guild was carrying out on their human guinea pigs, he waited impatiently to see how his fellow humans would react to these programs. He thought of his entitled position in society as a front row seat from which to closely observe the vast social, economic and lifestyle movements that were being orchestrated by his secret guild. He looked forward to watching the dust being kicked up and to seeing which people would come out on top and which would be left behind. With the quiet position his father had gotten him at an international bank after college, Richard would be able to watch these developments closely as a member of both the financial/banking elite as well as the secret guild.

Time passed, the programs moved rapidly ahead, and Richard's curiosity about the effects of these programs gradually turned into weariness and worse. He groped for perspective and answers. He had already started out in a dark place thanks to the heaviness of his surroundings, the obsessions of his father and secret society associates, and the drain from the negative entities that had hovered around him for so much of his life. However watching the evil experiments and forced indoctrinations imposed by his ruling cohorts succeed time and time again as a sheep-like humanity unquestioningly knuckled under to all that was demanded of them eventually left Richard without even a glimmer of hope. It had gotten to the point, he heard, where even the ruling families and their secret societies were shocked at how much they were getting away with and how quickly and easily everything was moving along. Aside from a few groups of awakened people who were easily marginalized anyway, there was nothing at all coming back at them in response to the ever more draconian measures rammed into place by them. There was only complete, mind-numbing passivity. Ironically, the only time most people got riled up at all was when the few folks who were aware tried to warn them about what was going on. Apparently the only thing the masses could not tolerate was any real criticism of the system to which they were now attached as if by an umbilical cord.

As depressing and life-disaffirming as Richard found all of this, he gradually came to an even darker realization. Over the years he had studied abuse extensively from both sides. He had been thoroughly trained on how to be an abuser from his father and his secret guild and while in college he had also studied abuse from the many books and programs that had become available from the victim's or survivor's perspective. From this unique combination of experience and research, Richard understood how the truly evil abuser not only forced his way with his victims during the abusive event, whatever it might be, but he also did something that was much worse. Over time, this worst of all abusers slowly and methodically groomed his victims into willingly participating in his abuse of them. He led them

136

step by step down a dark path towards accepting as normal his ever more invasive intrusions. Behaviors and situations that the victim would have instinctively found reprehensible beforehand became somehow acceptable and permissable after this careful cultivation. Thus on top of whatever forms the abuse itself took, such abusers also methodically destroyed their victims' dignity, will power and sense of self – often permanently. Nothing beats a person or a people down more than having willingly agreed to their own abuse and oppression.

Richard realized that so successfully had the dark planners slowly groomed the public into accepting their programming, they could now take away peoples' rights and resources at a moment's notice with little to no resistance. Just about everything was in place. That much was plain to see. It was only a question of timing now for when the dark planners would make their next big move.

How had they gotten so far? What form had the grooming taken over these last years to get the people to where they were now? How was something so far reaching so invisible? How had he not even seen it himself? For his own edification, Richard decided to trace back the steps, find the underlying patterns and come to a deeper understanding of how it had come about. He settled on starting his research around the time of the watershed 9/11 event that had taken place in his own country. Understanding the significance of that event and moving forward from there would go a long way towards helping him tease the latest grooming patterns apart from the general background of daily detail, chaos and public spin.

The modern day system was a massive illusion. Richard already knew that. It was all a big play, a real life movie produced and directed by Richard's secret guild and starring everyone else. The so-called call to arms, the war cry of "9/11" was one of the most significant and best orchestrated plot lines of recent history. It was delivered with a complex back story created by the secret guild and pushed out through their intelligence agency minions.

To usher in this plot line, they had already developed a fake enemy advertised as "terrorists" who they implicated in a number of violent events around the world. The fairly well organized terrorist groups which commanded so many headlines were generally nothing but a group of opportunists at the top and desperate or unbalanced mentally ill people at the bottom. Perhaps some religious fanatics were thrown into the groups for good measure but no matter who was in them, Richard learned that these groups had ultimately been created by and were controlled by his secret guild.

At carefully orchestrated moments, secret guild cronies who were strategically placed throughout many governments were prompted by their demonic inner voices to order the so-called terrorist groups to start participating in "false flag" terror attacks on the citizens of the ruling families' own countries. The events themselves were quietly choreographed by stealthy government groups but were publicly pinned on terrorist groups. Indeed prior to 9/11, a number of these staged events had already taken place here and there and seemingly from time to time. Over several years, the timing of these events built in frequency and momentum. They mounted in worldwide publicity until a mighty crescendo of sudden false flag violence burst upon the world one autumn day and catapulted the game to a new level of play.

So well prepared for and managed was this particular event that the ripple effect was felt around the world instantly. So well prepared for and managed was 9/11 that the vital step of incrementally stripping citizens around the globe of critical liberties was swiftly set in motion without a flaw. Indeed, heinous laws were passed and discomfiting restrictions enacted so quickly that it was almost as if the necessary machines and laws and personnel had been ready and waiting for just this opportunity. In this Richard recognized the stamp of his guild. When the new laws, restrictions and practices were being floated out to the public, they were touted as only applying to those deadly and unpredictable terrorists. Once the ink dried, however, they turned out to apply to all citizens. They applied to average citizens as well as babies and old people, unimportant government officials and movie stars, the sick and infirm, business travelers and students, workers of every kind, farmers and writers. All were included in their net and the net kept getting pulled tighter and tighter.

As Richard traced this along, he saw that on the heels of the legal net tightening in defense against foreign terrorists there came a new surge of carefully timed and staged terrorist attacks. This time, though, the attacks were attributed to domestic terrorist related groups. These domestic groups were said to be filled with rabble rousers who were fighting for "freedom" and "survival" and were filled with soldiers and "patriots." It didn't matter, though, because these domestic groups too were controlled by the secret guild, if they even existed at all as actual groups.

Most of the members of Richard's secret guild did not consciously understand the complex system of grooming and abuse they were engaged in. They were going along with what had become normal life to them just like everyone else did. They did not question; they did not observe. It was just the way things were and they played their respective roles like automatons. However, Richard was different. He never did go completely to sleep. He watched. He considered. He could look back and see that each attack had clearly had a specific purpose. With each attack, the masses lost another level of their civil liberties. With each attack, more wealth was taken from the poor and given to the rich. With each attack, the earthbound humans' slave bonds became stronger and more deeply embedded in their minds. Richard could easily see the pattern in detail now and understand the method of the grooming. He could trace its malevolent web of relationships and planned events and sound bites. It was all there – the force and the capitulations, the dangerous reworking of society under the guise of keeping everyone safe.

Now Richard could watch the march of events in the present with greater understanding as the grooming process was kicking up another notch. After 9/11, the time had been ripe for the masses to lose a big chunk of their personal sovereignty. Step one was for their victims to learn to give in to personal intrusions at a place that was foreign to them. The people needed to be a little uncomfortable and off balance for this step to be successful. When people are at home, they feel stronger and more independent. They know what constitutes normal behavior. But when people are traveling, they are already volunteering to go outside of their comfort zone. They tend to open themselves up to new experiences. They are willing to suspend adhering to what is normal for them and relax their boundaries in a way that they ordinarily would not. So the villains picked airports as the perfect place to launch their new initiative.

Once the venue had been chosen, the evil planners set in motion a series of well thought out phases that had been years in the planning. Each phase fulfilled its own special purpose in removing a layer of defense from the people and in chipping away at the public's sense of dignity and control over even their own bodies. Each phase was pushed through based upon the manufactured mass fear that "those terrorists" might strike at any time. Each phase was designed to take away the masses' ability to say "no."

First the dark planners trotted out a shoe bomber who was said to have boarded a plane wearing shoes packed with explosives in order to blow it up. After this event, new airport procedures were put in place that required everyone to take off an article of clothing, i.e., their shoes, while going through airport security. People quickly acquiesced to this with no problem as taking your shoes off was not big deal. So next the dark planners staged another bomb attack in which the fake perpetrators were supposedly going to mix together a bomb from over-the-counter liquids while in flight. With this, the abusers proclaimed that in order to keep everyone safe in the air, they had to minutely search the luggage of all passengers and restrict what liquids could be brought on board even including drinking water. Again the public gave in without so much as a whimper. With this, the abusers had established being able to go through their victims' belongings and throw out things they claimed were dangerous in ways known only to them. Also the abusers were now in a position to dictate to their victims which items they could and could not travel with. So two more levels of boundaries had now been successfully breached and removed from the victims' defense system.

Finally came the phase that would complete the airport-based portion of the grooming sequence. Once a shoe bomber had proved to be so useful, an underwear bomber could not be far behind. The specialists that carried out this particular fake terrorist operation botched it horribly but Richard noticed that it didn't seem to matter at all. Even though the mistakes and changed stories around this event were so numerous that it was easy for many people to spot this as a government sponsored operation, the government was still able to effortlessly roll out the use of what Richard knew as the infamous "naked body scanners." Within days of the underwear bomber false flag, what the government called full-body scanners became mandatory at airports around the world. A number of these new and costly scanners had just been manufactured and they were ready and waiting to be deployed at a moment's notice. This convenient timing looked so suspicious that even the media that was owned and largely run by the abusers started to ask some questions about it. How could these scanners be manufactured just in time for the aftermath of the underwear bomber? Obviously without the underwear bomber event, no one would have accepted these scanners. Could this all be a coincidence?

It all looked so contrived that even the pacified public started to give some push back about this new system of airport security. Richard read article after article and saw video after video expressing outrage and condemnation of these scanners that radiated their victims and profoundly invaded their privacy. It seemed that people had finally been pushed too far and were going to say "No!" It turned out, though, that humanity's ability to defend itself was apparently not that strong. The abusers just let everything cool down for a while and then implemented the mandatory use of naked body scanners anyway, simply ignoring any resistance and backing up the blanket use of these scanners with strong laws, punitive measures and forceful personnel.

Within a few short years, the public allowed themselves and their children to be photographed by these scanners and touched in inappropriate ways by strange staff. When parents brought even young children to the airport, they faced two choices. The first choice was to have their children radiated and photographed as if naked by strangers. The only alternative choice was to allow strangers to physically grope their children's private parts, even to the extent of removing diapers in the supposed search for weapons. In either case, parents watched helplessly as government-backed strangers essentially sexually abused their children. In short, Richard could see that people had conceded all of these personal liberties without as much as a whimper in the interest of safety. Clearly things had now gone so far for so long that no one could say "no" any longer. "No", even with respect to intimate touch and search and seizure of private property, was no longer an option. Thus the airport portion of the grooming of their victims had been successfully completed by the secret guilds and their families. Now the way was open for them to expand this grooming, this twisting of modern life, into areas of life beyond airports.

Richard continued to trace the pattern. There were a few more faked minor domestic terror attacks and one major one, at which point the dark planners were able to declare that all people were potential terrorists. As this new idea of imminent and present danger circulated through society, the secret guilders shoehorned all of the abusive behaviors and procedures they had established at airports into every other aspect of their citizens' lives. Authorities were now empowered to raid people's homes and rifle through their belongings. They were able to stop people at random check points and pat them down and scan them as a matter of course. The worst kinds of thugs and degenerates were hired to these kinds of law enforcement and security positions. Sadistic, pedophilic lowlifes flocked in to be a part of this new style of police force. Before too long, the searching of belongings became looting and the pat downs became groping and even worse. The people had left their "no" at the airport after all. By now these abusive behaviors were accepted as normal and they were backed by law. The tables had turned so utterly that when people did sometimes object to such invasive and violent treatment, they were the ones labeled as hostile. They were the troublemakers who were resisting normal, acceptable behavior for no apparent reason. Worse, "troublemakers" could easily morph into "terrorists" and be made into most unfortunate examples.

Richard stepped back for a bit and considered. Based on this long view of the patterns of change implemented by the dark lords in just the last decade or so, what was happening now after so many years of their grooming and restructuring of society? Well now that that this level of abuse had become the established norm and against a background of economic chaos and social disruption, the coveted martial law had at long last been ordered and was slowly falling into place. It was now ingrained that all citizens were potential terrorists with no civil liberties. They didn't actually own property and they had no rights. They were really all prisoners and slaves and were increasingly being openly treated as such. Citizens could be taken to death camps to be taken out of circulation or exterminated or they could be taken away to provide slave labor. It was all happening.

Getting all of this into perspective and then watching the current horror show develop from the protected isolation of his gated community of other secret guilders and his office at the bank shocked Richard to his core. Then one very important day it dawned on him that the leaders, his secret brethren, were themselves being groomed. He remembered that after his initiation into his secret guild, he was told that many of the abusive behaviors his group practiced had been taught to them by extra-terrestrials. He realized that his group was just doing the bidding of the otherworld overlords. He could suddenly see it as clear as day. The purpose of his group was to pacify and enslave the masses so that the extraterrestrials could eventually come down and enslave not only those masses but his cohorts as well. Now that he was so conscious of the pattern, he could put it together with his knowledge of the history of his secret guild and see that the same patterns and the same training tools had been used all along on his group of dark planners as his group of dark planners had in turn used on the rest of the population of the planet. This was just the same old pattern of victims turning into the next generation of abusers that he had seen play out in individual lives over and over again. Now that he thought about it, he realized that the initiation process into his secret guild was itself a complex system of grooming and abuse. A hundred confirming details unfolded before his eyes. For instance, within his guild, every member policed every other member by using the threat of being ostracized by their loved ones and associates if exposed. In this way and many other abusive ways, the whole secret guild system was held together at every level by each individual pressuring the secret guild members around them to toe the line.

With this new perspective uppermost in his mind, Richard tentatively started asking the higher up's of his secret clan about the grooming they had undergone. He also started to question his peers about this. Some members responded by growing angry and sarcastic with him. Others looked scared and bewildered. Richard reasoned that each of his guild members were only in charge of a small piece of the puzzle and so could not see the whole picture. It was purposely designed that way. He would only ever be able to get so many answers from any of them. No one, except one key member, looked like they had any idea of what Richard was talking about.

When Richard finally asked his father if their alien bene-factors were merely using the secret guild as a means of furthering their own secret plan, a brief look of confirmation flickered across Adrian's face before he turned away without answering. So Richard's father knew. He was obviously specially connected to these alien overlords somehow. Richard had his answer.

It was then that Richard finally saw that he would have to make a choice. He would either have to join with these extraterrestrial overlords in enslaving humanity or he would have to die like the rest of humanity. He was not yet aware that someday he would discover a third option.

22. Those Poor Americans

Having studied the complexities of human beings for many centuries, the Great Usurpers had already known ahead of time that they were going to need an experimental population upon which to test what would be the apotheosis of their grand experiment. Their plans had been moved forward all over the globe very nicely but they were still going to need a controlled environment within which to subject a selected population to a complete separation from the divinity within them. They had to see exactly what would happen since human beings had surprised them before. Of all the countries of the world, what would later be called the United States had been chosen by them for this experimentation. Long before this particular region had been fortuitously invaded by Europeans, the Great Usurpers had calculated what was going to be required to create a "United States" that would serve their needs. Well ahead of time, they had designed every aspect of its future government and society according to the specifications of their massive experiment.

The land that would be the United States was one of incomparable wealth. It was vast and contained large percentages of the world's fresh water, wood, and many other natural resources. The indigenous people who already lived there were themselves extraordinary for their strength and abilities but the Great Usurpers had come up with a plan for dealing with them well in advance. The Usurpers needed to clear this land out so that they could start from scratch and build upon it an unprecedented society, government and economy that would exactly suit their purposes. The machinations of how the Great Usurpers engineered this dramatic change of who lived on this land and how they lived on this land filled many history books, although none included the essential truth that it had all been engineered towards carrying out this insidious experiment. In any case, the Great Usurpers created a United States designed to be easy to manipulate, and they worked diligently to remake the population into the dependent slave population they were looking for.

In due course after the arrival of the Europeans, the powerful natives of the land became worse than dead. In a surprisingly short period of time, they were replaced by an incoming swarm of diverse ethnicities of people from all over the earth who were lured to this "new land" by promises of wealth and freedom. This new group became the foundation for the Great Usurpers' new test population, a population never before seen on the earth. Everywhere the word went out that this new country was a gold mine and a utopia. So for centuries people left everything behind – their culture, their lifestyle, their families, their land, their history – and got themselves to America for the express purpose of getting ahead, of getting a new deal, of getting a fresh start in a fabulously richly endowed country. Their dreams and ambitions allowed them to see this new country as the future for all mankind. They believed in the United States. They believed in the American dream with all that they had. They had risked everything to come to this country and so they poured themselves into this new land completely. The new people's extreme willingness to adjust and their deep hunger for wealth and change made them the best possible test subjects for the experiment.

During Richard's time, minions at the various intelligence agencies around the world who secretly, and in most cases unknowingly, worked for the Great Usurpers called the type of experiment the Great Usurpers were creating a "psyop" or psychological operation. It could have been called a "black op" as well because of its malevolent and dark nature. It was, in fact, both. Project America was a massive, malevolent, psychological operation designed to manipulate every aspect of every American's life from birth to death towards a very specific purpose.

By modern times, the American social system had been so well organized that the test subjects of the Great Usurpers' experiment were formally introduced to their controlled environment at birth itself for the birth of an American child had been made into a very high-tech affair. The natural, time honored system for human birth was the same as the system for all mammals. It ideally took place in a dark, safe, quiet haven with only a few loved ones around for support, if necessary, and a wise woman or midwife. The mother and baby were left alone afterwards to reconnect and bond after their relationship had gone through such a major transition from the inside of the mother to the outside world. It is a very pivotal time in the life of the baby and for the relationship between the mother and child. It is a time for quiet and sensitivity as the mother lets the child know that she is as present as ever. There should be no interventions or disruptions at this time, unless there are life threatening circumstances, as nothing is more important to the child and its mother than this sacred time that will define both of them in so many ways physically, emotionally and spiritually. This time defines how the child will perceive the world and how the mother will create a bubble around her baby that replaces the womb as the nurturing force that envelops the child's existence. If this transitional time is impeded in any way, the child begins to doubt. The child feels insecure and unsafe. The child does not trust that its needs are going to be met. It feels alone and unprotected. This is the case if there is even the slightest interruption between the mother and the child at this pivotal time after birth. In the psyop that was the American system, this relationship was not just interrupted. It was immediately prevented from being fully formed, or being formed at all, for the first act of this system had to be to cut the child and the mother off from each other.

The objective of this black psyop so carefully designed by the Great Usurpers was to take everything natural, simple and divine in the human being and in human life and replace it with a mechanical, bureaucratic, heavy, loveless, materially-based modification. The many, many modifications that they used to reshape modern life were all designed to pull people away from their hearts and towards a fractured, technological way of life. This way of life now formed the entire world of almost every

American on every level from start to finish of their lives.

The entire Usurper-designed system, particularly modern-day Project America, was so well designed with redundancies behind every door and curtain that not every aspect of their operation had to be experienced sequentially by each individual American for each stage to still be effective for the Great Usurpers had discovered that not every intervention, alteration or bit of programming had to be experienced by each individual for the mass effect to still hold sway. While there were multiple avenues through which each stage could be successfully completed, it turned out that human nature was such that for any one person who did not become fully indoctrinated during one of the stages, the desire to be like everyone else finished the job anyway. So it ended up not mattering that some people here and there were not forced through the artificial system like everyone else. As the majority of people were effectively forced through it, a sort of herd effect was in operation at all times much to the delight of the Great Usurpers.

For the time of birth, it was arranged that there would be so many violent interventions and barriers thrown up between the mother and her child that it would be next to impossible for families to fight them all off. Just during the months leading up to the birth, the pregnant mother was subjected to sufficient hostile energies, medicines and intrusions that she was often left dazed and disconnected before the birth even took place. Interventions during the birth itself became too many to even list and took place in an environment that was itself an intervention, i.e. in hospitals. Heavy duty pain medications administered during labor left both mother and baby sleepy and disoriented after the birth. In many, many cases the birth process was done away with altogether by simply cutting the mother open and unceremoniously pulling the baby out instead. These surgical births left the many natural reactions and hormonal cascades normally activated by the baby exiting the womb dangerously inactivated. Whether by the use of heavily medicated birth or surgical birth, the life affirming contact and bonding meant to take place during the critical post-birth hours was dramatically undermined, if not made impossible, by the forceful conditions imposed at birth. The machinery and lights, the drugs and chemicals, the rules and uniformed staff, and the heavy vibrations of hospitals left mothers and babies in a state of shock. Indeed the whole family unit was left in a state of shock by this birth process so carefully engineered by the Usurpers and their human cronies.

Once the baby was finally born, it was quickly scooped up and passed off to medical strangers who poked, pricked, prodded and stabbed it with syringes. Vaccines were immediately administered to the brand new baby. These vaccines were cocktails of chemicals, bits of diseases, heavy metals, and diluted toxins which went deep into the systems of these babies whose immune systems were not yet even activated. Their bodies' ability to ever say no to microscopic invaders was short circuited within the first few hours of life. If the baby were a male child, then the most sensitive part of its body was routinely mutilated within hours or days of birth. These circumcisions, which had become much more severe in modern times than from when this practice had been first introduced, laid the ground for the future deadening of sensitivity and increasingly aggressive attitudes and behaviors in the society's men. In most cases, babies were taken away from the mother and placed in a plastic cubicle in another room. Contained in these boxes, they were cut off completely from the warmth and love that all babies and all people need to thrive and succeed in this world. "Welcome to America, kid."

So, in broad strokes, this was the child's first introduction to the world and to the psyop that was the American system. The child (and the parents) learned early that it was the system that called the shots in the child's life and not the parents. As the child (and the parents) grew, it learned that the system could do whatever it wanted with the child and that the parents could do very little about it. Experiencing this reality and watching its parents try to function within this reality was the child's foundational education in its role of slave to the system.

In fact throughout childhood, the child and the parents still maintained a relationship with each other but the Great Usurpers' system was always in the middle of that relationship directing it in many important ways. At the outset, parents were instructed to train their child to sleep in a cage. The practice of placing a young one in a box or crib and letting it cry itself to sleep until it finally gave up and learned to go to silently to sleep alone was not found anywhere in nature except in modern human homes. Not only did no other mammal force its young to sleep separately from its mother, but within the more highly evolved mammals mothers and offspring were inseparable for at least the first couple of years of life. Even the most vicious of predators nurtured their newborns through the first few phases of life. Critical information is transmitted through the close physical contact of early life that is essential to the successful development of the young and the continuation of the species. No, such a pernicious practice was introduced into latter day American culture by the Great Usurpers and for a very specific reason.

In the black op/psychological experiment that became America, the flow of essential information from person to person, from heart to heart, and from one plane of existence to another had to be blocked at all costs in order for the Usurpers' plans to be successful. It was imperative, then, that mother and child be physically separated as soon as possible. In nature when a mother hears her offspring crying, she always rushes to it and takes care of its needs. In modern day America such moment to moment care and attention became frowned upon. It was said to breed weakness in the child. Rather parents were trained to use cribs, strollers, playpens, bottles, pacifiers, TV's and videos, schedules and daycare arrangements of all descriptions in order to enforce the necessary distance between mother and child and, eventually, between family and child. Parents and children alike suffered but the system worked. The natural connection between mother and father and child was severely damaged. Typically, the

151

child shut down and looked elsewhere for comfort and support. The mother's ability to intuit what her child needed was weakened as was her confidence. She had been duped into trusting a hostile system rather than what she knew inside of herself to be best for her child. Fathers too lost confidence in their ability to discern what was true and protect their families from hostile takeovers. Such losses of confidence were crippling and made the family limp along at best.

The damaged and weakened family could no longer protect the vulnerable child who was then easily stripped of its remaining shields and boundaries. This was accomplished first by getting the child away from the family and into the world as soon as possible and, secondly, by training the child to seek the fulfillment of its most primary desires through the allures of the material world. In other words, the child was rushed out into society and conditioned into becoming a consumer. Aggressive and intrusive marketing systems were developed in this American experiment to specifically target children and steer them away from seeking fulfillment through relationships and skill-building and towards seeking fulfillment through the acquisition of toys, treats, clothes, electronics and other material goods.

Why was it so important to turn these experimental children into deeply entrenched consumers and "system dwellers"? Some observers of the time warned that the system was headed towards making people into slaves. They had no idea who had really created the system and so had no way of knowing that the goal of the system didn't stop with making people into slaves but was actually far more horrifying than that. The truth was that the majority of earthbound humans were already slaves in one way or another as molding them into that mentality had long ago been a stepping stone for the Great Usurpers towards their larger plans. As a matter of fact, when the Usurpers had later brought up a class of earthbound dark planners to manage operations on Earth for them, they had inculcated in their planners a deep attachment to having slaves themselves. So now the dark planners managed a vast slave population for their own comfort, enjoyment and power while the Usurpers managed both the dark planners and the earthbound humans in order to eventually extract something even more precious.

So unbeknownst to the dark planners, this meant that there was actually a great divide between them and their source of direction and power, the Great Usurpers. Where the dark planners wanted earthbound humans strong enough to be workers, the Great Usurpers wanted them weak enough to be suppliers of soul energy. The dark planners used to want humans strong of body, bound in chains, and forced through fear and torture to physically work for their slave masters. Now, with changing times and evolving plans, they wanted humans weak of body but strong in their abilities with technology and State approved work. Either way, the dark planners wanted workers. But again, the Great Usurpers wanted souls. Earthbound humans were created as slaves and generally had been slaves throughout their long and tumultuous history. That is why the concept of "freedom" had always meant so much to them. By now, the Usurpers did not have to work at keeping them as slaves. No, now they were bent on devolving earthbound humans lower than that into mere materials to be stripped and rearranged at their will. In other words, they were moving earthbound humans from the status of slave down to the status of prey.

Therefore, the Great Usurpers had devised a new system for shuttling earthbound humans along into the next phase they had planned for them. This new system was layered upon the old slave system like icing on a cake. They simply gave the old system of external pressures and motivations, force and abuse a twist so that the earthbound humans living in Project America would become slaves not just of outer masters but of their own inner desires. To accomplish this, the Usurpers relentlessly squeezed Americans (particularly the young ones) into a lifestyle of consuming which constantly fanned the flames of their desires until they were unquenchable. This way, the Usurpers could use the Americans' overwhelming desire to consume as motivation for enthusiastically participating in this new devolution into becoming mere bits and pieces. By stimulating their prey's base drives for pleasure, stimulation, sugar, salt, fat, sex, power, money, control and security while at the same time weakening their bodies, minds, wills, relationships and inner connections with themselves, nature and the divine within, the Great Usurpers had been making great strides in getting earthbound humanity into just the right state required for the ultimate harvest.

The more Americans indulged, the more they wanted and the deeper into the system they plunged. Instead of outward chains, their bondage was now inside of them and growing stronger every day. As they became increasingly dependent upon and addicted to this system of satiation, they also came to a place where they could only see the system as good. They vociferously fought anyone who said otherwise or who threatened the system in any way. They believed utterly that they were free without realizing that this closely held belief left them no avenue of escape. To keep the whole delusion going, it was imperative that over time new children were constantly and forcefully molded into addicts of their own desire-based consumption habits. To keep that going, the children had to be taken away from their families as soon as possible.

The Great Usurpers discovered early on that loving relationships threw all kinds of monkey wrenches into their system so they found endless ways to throw monkey wrenches into loving relationships. For instance, children were directed away from the intimate embrace of their families as early in life as possible. This was rationalized with the only reason that could possibly be a strong enough one – "necessity". Indeed, the necessity of moving young children out of the family sphere and into the embrace of the State was so effectively engineered out of thin air that parents not only agreed to it but accepted it, usually gratefully. There was little fuss or push back. And what was this necessity? Economics, of course. It was the necessity of survival

154

in this experimental modern life created by the Great Usurpers. In order to keep (consuming) body and (imperiled) soul together, mothers and fathers both had to work away from home full time in order to earn the money it took to live in the way they were told they must live. The State was there to raise the child in the best possible and most scientific way in the meantime. This was a perfect arrangement all the way around. The Great Usurpers congratulated themselves. Now children spent their days at government run schools and the rest of their time submersed in some form of isolating, mind-numbing technology. As the years of their childhoods passed in this manner, the connection between the children and their families was almost completely broken. Herds of children were thoroughly indoctrinated by the controllers of the psyop and modern children were easily maneuvered into keeping each other in line through relentless peer pressure from other equally indoctrinated children. As most parents had been pretty thoroughly indoctrinated as well, the children had no source for real information or an outside perspective. In any case, children were trained to resist their parents' teachings and authority so even if the parents had understood what was happening, their children would not have taken them seriously anyway.

As a matter of fact by the time children had grown into their adolescence during this modern period of Project America, they had already been tightly scripted to lose all respect for their parents. A hostile relationship between parents and adolescents became a culturally expected and sanctioned phenomenon. The modern techniques parents were taught to use for raising their children had been designed and suggested in order to sabotage the parent-child relationship. Modern parents were no longer even able to detect that their relationships with their children were deteriorating so they blindly followed what they were told was the best way, the modern way, to handle their children. As a result, modern-day children were largely left to raise themselves. The State had free rein. With the loss of authority and lack of intimacy that now characterized parent-child relationships, parents looked weak in their children's eyes. Impotent parents with no effective way to discipline or teach their children were pretty much left with only one tactic to use – they could threaten or bribe their children. They could give or withhold material possessions. They could use the very material possessions created by the controllers of the experiment for controlling their children who were already being manipulated by the controllers of the experiment. Parents were drawn into using on their children the very materials and inducements that had been designed to weaken them and isolate them from each other. At this point in the experiment, what passed for harmony in the family was generally established by acquiring lots of things as the desire arose and spending large chunks of time while at home separately interfacing with electronic devices. The quiet of individual hypnotic states had become the new family harmony.

In conjunction with this, in order to create exploitable emotional instability, children were routinely subjected to massive amounts of unnatural stimuli long before they were developmentally ready to process it. They lived their lives immersed in carefully constructed, rapidly shifting visual stimuli that unsettled their brains to such an extent that it actually permanently changed the way their brains functioned. They were introduced to adult level experiences at a young age as well. They were sexualized culturally long before it was developmentally appropriate. Through music, TV shows, video games, modern books and movies, they were bombarded with violence and dark and dreary worlds. The myriad ways of robbing children of their childhood and innocence were many and very effective. Within less than a generation, children's minds and emotions were breaking down at epidemic levels.

The Great Usurpers' experiment was designed to make the American people passive and malleable on one level but socially competitive and aggressive on another. To encourage this, children and young people were taught to compete with their

156

siblings and peers for attention, resources and approval. They were taught to have a killer instinct and a "go out and grab it" approach to life. They were taught to never question the authority of the State, their peers or advertising but yet to disrespect the authority of their parents or their own hearts. They were taught to get aggressive if they felt personally wronged by another person or family member but to accept any and all violations to their collective rights and liberties by the controlling entities. They were stripped of all meaningful rites of passage and any personal connection to nature. Rather their time and passages were now marked in nanoseconds and by credit card receipts. Young people, in particular, were fed a carefully measured diet of mixed messages within a stripped down, anchorless life. The end results were stunning. By now, the American adolescent was basically lost. They were disconnected from everything within and outside of themselves that was natural, healthy and appropriate for earthbound humans.

Even so a window of opportunity for freedom could still open when the natural process of individuation that began in adolescence and ended in adulthood kicked in. During that time there was a possibility that some of the youth might break through their programming and take steps to shake it off altogether. The Usurpers who had dissected the human psyche for so many years were aware of this and had already launched several strategies to counter this unfortunate possibility in their experiment.

One strategy involved provoking and channeling teenage anger and rebellion at their parents, other peer groups, individuals in authority and any people different from the youth. The whole society had long since been purposively divided up into all kinds of cliques, classes, political parties, social groups, languages, races, religions, sports franchises and castes. Rebellious young people were steered towards tightly identifying themselves with one or more of these groups and encouraged to hate the opposing groups. This hate was portrayed as natural and right so young people were easily directed towards venting their anger and rebellion at those other groups in society.

Another effective strategy for warding off any possible "awakening" in adolescents was to convince them that everything was just a joke. Life was a party. Life was purely about enjoyment, sensual pleasure, and immediate gratification. Having been sexualized at too early an age, young people now had little to no restraint or moderation with regards to pleasurable activities by the time they were adolescents. Ceaseless advertising showed them that it was their god-given right to have fun and god help anyone who got in the way of their good time. So they squandered their youthful opportunities, energy, and time indulging in all sorts of ridiculous things. Even good shows of rebellion became nothing but indulgences as by now they never amounted to anything more than a lot of talk and showboating. For obvious reasons, then, "rebellions" of this time never included actually confronting the system that provided them with so much fabricated, unadulterated pleasure.

The corporatized media and ever advancing technological achievements came to play a key role in the Great Usurpers' methodologies for this modern phase of their experiment. For instance, through the widespread use of media devices such as computers, TVs and cell phones, the Great Usurpers were able to program and track their test subjects with great specificity. As their subjects – the American people – stared at these pieces of equipment day after day, their brains slipped from the active beta-wave state to the passive alpha-wave state. Once they had entered into the suggestible alpha-wave state, they became highly impressionable and programmable.

Radio and TV had successively put older generations in a trance and told them straight out how to live, what to believe in, what to wear, what they should look and smell like, what to eat, what to enjoy, what was up and what was down. TV shows were even commonly referred to as "programming" which was ironic as they actually were used to program the subjects of the experiment. One of the chief ways humans learned was through observation and imitation so TV shows conveniently provided curricula for both. As the years had passed, TV programs and movies had introduced increasingly graphic images into the psyches of the population. Plus the characters in movies and shows of all types were portrayed with poorer and poorer morals. They treated each other with more and more hostility. They were increasingly immature, selfish, coarse, vulgar and entitled. Young people in particular modeled their behavior, characters and attitudes on these freely available training videos. This programming went a long, long way towards blocking unwanted questioning in them or any tendency towards shaking off the parameters of the experiment.

As technology continued to advance, the Great Usurpers were able to increase the intensity and subtlety of their bombardment of their test population. Americans could now be trained in the realities of violent and primitive alternative worlds through video games, for instance. At least as significant, Americans spent endless hours every day on computers, cell phones and other technological devices until finally most of their social contacts were made through these electronic devices rather than face to face. Eventually they forgot how to easily and sincerely communicate even with loved ones without a device of some kind between them and the other person. Young people particularly but gradually almost everybody carried devices with them wherever they went. This is what the Usurpers wanted so that people could be told what to do wherever they were at all times of day or night and so that they could be tracked. By Richard's time, people were lost without them. He observed that this transformation had taken place so seamlessly and with such greedy approval by the dependent population that no one had even noticed what it was costing them.

Years passed and what had frankly become called "social media" was further refined and taken to yet another level. Whenever people received their next hit of programming from the system, they constantly and voluntarily told their friends all about their reactions to that programming. They all compulsively discussed everything about it on the social media. This provided the Great Usurpers and their dark planners with extremely useful data. Enormous quantities of this data were collected and analyzed to provide crucial feedback as to how well the people were integrating their programming. The majority of people volunteering data on the one side while the controlling few mined that data on the other became the way of life for everybody concerned. Every aspect of the lives of Americans was almost instantly analyzed. This allowed the controllers to fine-tune the programming and deepen their level of control as well as search for patterns that would help them find creative new ways to weaken their human subjects.

That search for patterns that would lead to new ways of weakening the earthbound humans was what was most closely monitored in all of the data that came pouring in. The controlled environment of the psyop was saturated with low level combinations of drugs, poisons, toxins, genetic alterations, radiation, subliminal messages, low grade energetic waves that interfered with human functioning, and other elements that subverted the test subjects' natural processes. Americans were under constant assault on every level of their being. It was important that the controllers be able to closely follow exactly how all of these inputs were affecting their subjects. The goal was to steadily weaken them – not kill them – in gradual ways that would be accepted by the people with minimal effort from the controllers.

Throughout the time of the implementation of all of these subversive changes, the Americans steadfastly believed that they were a free people. In reality, however, they only ever had one choice and that was to remain a subject, a guinea pig, in the Usurpers' experiment. The Usurpers' controlled psyop was their whole world. They felt lost when they were outside of that sterile, controlled environment. They were afraid of natural life. They were afraid of the natural functions of their own minds and

160

bodies. They were afraid of germs, insects, soil, the sun, animals and even other people who were not found within their tight circle of familiarity. They lived in houses sprayed with poisons to keep all forms of life out. They were told complex lies about how natural life was unsafe and caused disease. They were so weak that they needed the temperature around them to remain constant at all times. They needed their bath water always hot and their food always packaged.

The truth was that they had lost practically everything as human beings, as sovereign creatures. They had lost their natural survival instincts. They had lost their families and villages. They had lost their agrarian skills. They had lost their many abilities to connect with the world around them and within them. They were angry, had no tolerance for pain or challenges, had an extremely short attention span, could not think clearly or feel deeply, and had little tolerance for hard work. They could neither lead nor follow. They all longed to be stars and recognized as special and yet they lacked any of the skills and inner resources required to make themselves so.

As the Great Usurpers predicted – in fact they were depending on this –the earthbound humans raised in America and confronted with such deterioration both within and without still clung to the earthbound human tendency towards "normalcy bias". They fiercely believed that everything they were going through and all that was being done to them was absolutely normal. No matter how extreme things became, they stoutly maintained that it was all normal and unavoidable. That left them with only one choice. They had to depend upon the very system that, unbeknownst to them, had been specifically created by their ancient enemies to bring them down.

Meanwhile this psyop did not come cheaply. It was so resource intensive to implement and run that most of the world's resources went into maintaining the experimental conditions known as America. But now, just as the physical Earth itself was at its own tipping point from being so thoroughly plundered and abused, the American subject population was exactly where the Usurpers and their minions wanted them to be. At last, it was time for the final phase of bringing down into rubble and ruin the entire artificial system they had created.

While the experiment was expressly set up in America, the long range goal was to harvest souls from the entire earthbound human population. The Project America experiment just made Americans the lead dogs of the Usurpers' master plan to usurp the position of God. It was the Americans who would lead the way towards the abyss of despair and agony waiting for all earthbound humans when their world came crumbling down. It was the Americans who would be the first to willingly hand their soul energy over to the Usurpers in exchange for a promise of just one more day in the matrix of the psyop. It was the Americans who felt so special and so sure that anything was possible within their world of illusion. It was they who would be the catalyst for the destruction of the world as they knew and the remaking of the Universe into the image of their ancient enemies. In this sense, the poor Americans were the chosen ones.

Americans were born and bred to believe in all things American. They believed in American ingenuity and American science and technology. They believed in the American spirit and in American infallibility and invincibility. They believed in America's leadership role in the world and in American peace. They believed in the unwritten promise that the American system was inherently good and would always take care of them. They believed that their system could never and would never fail them. They believed all of this so deeply that they sold this belief to practically everybody else on the planet. So when the American system was collapsed, the Great Usurpers knew that it would take the other systems around the world down with it. And when the system did finally collapse, the Americans would be sure that it was not their perfect system that was to blame. They would be compelled, then, to look for blame elsewhere.

One of the greatest weaknesses in the human being

which the appropriators had exploited mercilessly for millennia was that the people of Earth had a massive inferiority complex. Having been created and bred to be servants, slaves and "less thans" all the way around, they had a strong identification with a slave type of mentality. They had no idea of their true potential. For thousands of years, they had been genetically altered and mentally and socially manipulated. They had had devastating restrictions and limitations placed on their knowledge base, abilities and ways of life. In fact, throughout the whole of their history they had been told in one way or another, "There is something wrong with you. You are not okay. You are illegitimate." On top of this, earthbound humans had also made a lot of mistakes over the millennia. They had overindulged, been self-destructive and had operated from an overwhelming sense of guilt and shame foisted on them by religions and many other forces. The Usurpers capitalized on this by taking every opportunity to reinforce the earthbound humans' belief that they were not good enough.

At this late date in the history of the Usurpers' and earthbound humans' lives together, it was common for human genetics to contain a significant helping of Usurper genetics. As the Usurpers utterly loathed humans, earthbound humans often lived with debilitating self-hatred due to this genetic mash-up. It was kind of like putting snake genetics inside of rats. Some part of the rats' genetic makeup would be trying to devour itself from within.

The insidious strength of all of this conditioning and genetics was that even when the odd American did manage to experience a momentary awareness that it was the system itself that was poisoning them and everyone else, they just couldn't blame America. They did what earthbound humans have done for centuries. They blamed themselves. They often covered this self-blame up with false bravado and narcissism but deep down Americans always knew that they were the problem. They knew that they were the flaw in the system.

So this is what Richard was up against even within him-

163

self. He had had many lives which were failures. Over and over again his soul had returned to its resting place and undergone an unpleasant assessment of his performance in that last life. Like many other human beings, Richard had gotten into the habit of failing in his attempts to liberate himself from his earthly imprisonment. Many negative self-appraisals were etched in his soul. These identifying marks became obstacles and personality traits that carried over from life to life forming an uphill climb that he faced with every life.

Now in this life Richard carried the extra burden of the American psychological operation which had formed so much of his self-concept. In spite of the natural assumption of power and the accumulation of costly things by his father, like many other human beings and Americans in particular, Richard just did not believe that he deserved what was good in the world. In fact, a major hurdle for the Celestial Fellowship was getting the earthbound humans to believe that they were good enough, that they were legitimate, that they had abilities far beyond what they realized and that they had value. Humans in general needed to realize that they rightfully belonged with higher developed beings. They were not the low creatures that the Usurpers wanted them to believe that they were. It was imperative that humans come to understand and believe that they could ascend to the highest levels of spiritual advancement. It was imperative that they understand what a human life was really for and how to best think about the problems and difficulties that always arise in human lives. It was imperative that they learn to forgo their personal desires in order to selflessly serve in the ever changing work of the Divine Creator.

As the majority of humans did not understand any of these things yet and so could not have changed accordingly, they had not earned their rightful place in the Divine Hierarchy. The coming test that was about to be provided by the Great Usurpers would give them with an enormous opportunity to change, however. As their world collapsed around them, they would have

164

the chance to reach up and embrace their higher nature. They would have a chance to be reshaped and tempered into true strength. From this they would have a chance to earn their place in the stars.

Richard was no different in this regard. He too would have to fight off the negative tendencies he had brought with him into this life as well as the American training he had received. Even now, he had to remain balanced under the pain of the vibrations he felt from the wailing masses that surrounded him while simultaneously finding something in this world to still believe in. Most importantly, Richard had to find a way to believe in himself. It was game time for him. The world was about to plunge into free fall and America would fall faster and harder than anywhere else. The condition in America would be one of collective shock, anger, betrayal, madness and disbelief. Here in this country so centrally positioned in an interconnected world that was already unstable and that was being crushed under the pressure of a collapsing massive illusion, Richard would have to make his choice.

There was one saving grace for Richard in being in America. An essential aspect of the American mythos was that Americans could somehow accomplish anything in the end. The Usurpers had needed for Americans to have enough faith in "America" for the experiment to succeed. The fallout from this was that lurking in American psyches was the belief that a higher material destiny and potential for leadership was always within reach. It was a delusion of sorts, of course, but it was a source of hope and faith for Americans. The American experience was filled with stories of champions who had snatched victory out of the jaws of defeat or oblivion. Richard did not consciously realize it yet but he would be working toward becoming one of those champions.

23. The Law of Balance

It is hard to say whether or not the many upheavals that combined in their effect over the years to remake planet Earth and its earthbound populations were part of a universal script or not. It is true that many of the events were foreseen, and even orchestrated, by beings from other planes of existence. So in that sense the events were certainly not random. All of those who had a part in triggering them could even rightfully claim that they were only following the script and were, therefore, technically blameless. Beyond that, though, the catastrophic intensity of the upheavals was entirely a consequence of the many unnatural and blasphemous choices that had been made over thousands of years along the developmental path of the earthbound humans. In addition, choices had been made by evolved beings of all sorts on Earth too which had broken binding universal laws. This range of unlawful choices had created dense vibrational effects on Earth that had to be fully expressed in order to be released. In other words, the karma on Earth was heavy. This heavy grossness had to be cleansed from the planet, from its related energetic fields and from the people who inhabited it. At this point after the failure of many half measures aimed at correcting these negative developments on Earth, the only way for this cleansing to finally and sufficiently take place was through catastrophes and calamities of all sorts.

At the beginning of the upheaval phase, some of humanity could sense change. Something was brewing. Up to this point in remembered history, people had more or less flourished for years and years on a planet that was fairly stable, cooperative and supportive to life. There were the occasional earthly hiccups but, for the most part, it had been a long period during which humanity had flourished physically and materially. It might otherwise have been a time of expanding peace and unity too, but humanity had not set its sights on a world such as that. Instead their goals were selfish, self-destructive and almost entirely materialistic in nature. Of course the Great Usurpers' negative influence and the earthbound humans' genetic limitations did not help them to even consider becoming their best. Either way, earthbound humans were a very long way from reaching their highest potential.

As the centuries had gone by, the cumulative result of this vicious way of human life was that powerful and yet unconscious calls for change had gone up to the Creator over and over and over until they had reached a crescendo that had sparked a response. It was from their heart of hearts that the earthbound humans had put out this call as most of them were completely unaware of their inner craving for change. Once that call had been heard and received, however, latent forces were set into motion. Planet Earth began to shift and shudder.

On the human plane, Richard's secret guild's plans had not come into full swing quite yet but they were on the rise and gaining momentum. The dark planners as a whole were finally beginning their broad attempt at full global domination and complete subjugation of their earthly brothers and sisters. The Great Usurpers' plans too were coming to a head. They were now rushing to bring humanity to its knees so that they could get on with the experiment of stealing human souls.

The Earth itself was due to undergo some of its natural cleansing cycles at this time. Historically, these cycles were characterized by upheavals of various sorts anyway, occasionally enormous in size and scale. Tectonic plates might shift resulting in intense volcanic eruptions and widespread earthquakes. Weather patterns always changed dramatically. Solar flares typically increased in frequency and in intensity, triggering electrical and magnet changes on Earth. At the peak of very long cycles, the Earth's magnetic poles shifted. The shifting magnetic poles was such a large event that it marked the culmination of all of the upheavals of that period and the beginning of a new phase on Earth.

Elliptical cycles of this nature took place on every planet

167

in the solar system. Among other things, they served as a way to clear out unnatural and negative energy. They could be compared to a snake shedding its skin or to a person getting some sort of illness as they transition from one phase of life to another. Cleansing and transition phases exist everywhere in the universe. Planets, solar systems, stars and even the universe itself are not immune to such events. In fact, upheavals and apparent chaos are necessary at times to bring things back into balance and to move creation forward.

Contrary to what most earthbound humans believed, the point of balance in a living system is not a static or stationary point but rather is a subtle and gentle fluctuation back and forth within a narrow band on either side of the fulcrum. A balanced individual is not one who stands perfectly still at one particular point on their path of existence. That would be stagnation. No, a balanced person is one who continues to move forward on their spiritual path but leans slightly in one direction or the other as necessary as they proceed along it. They never lean so far as to unbalance themselves, but do lean just enough to allow them to follow the natural slope of the road as they walk. In this way, the path towards becoming what they are meant to become is followed in a natural, balanced, flexible manner. The balanced individual's range of movement is just right of center, center and just left of center. So over time they go through a cycle of being slightly out of balance to the right, completely on balance and then slightly out of balance to the left and the pattern goes on and on from there. Throughout this whole long process, they are never far from mathematical center.

If all of the people of Earth had operated (or even were operating now) in such a balanced fashion then the planet would not have gotten into the terrible state it was in. The already scheduled cleaning cycle the Earth was about to go through would have been far less intense and dramatic had that been the case. The condition that earthbound humans had created on their planet was very imbalanced, however. This worsening imbalance coupled with the fact that the Great Usurpers and the dark planners had been actively working to intensify the current cleaning and transitional earthly cycle for their own nefarious reasons would make this cycle the most chaotic in the planet's long history. The upheavals would be extremely intense and very dramatic but, mercifully, so would the opportunities for assuming personal responsibility and working on one's personal evolution.

For Lucy and Adrian, the law of balance represented different things to each of them in their personal work. This was especially true with regards to their work on their son Richard. While one of them was relying entirely on the law of balance to run its course and guide events towards the best, the other was counting on employing ancient techniques designed to subvert this universal principle and movement.

Lucy lived the law of balance. She herself resided in a balanced state in the center of her being as a matter of course. Her goal was to help her son, Neil, remember his true inner nature, thereby returning him to a more subtle balanced existence too. Adrian, on the other hand, resided on the extreme side of the dense world of materiality. He and his group could not withstand any movement back towards the center or, even worse, a swing towards the subtle spiritual world at the opposite pole of their existence. For him balance was not an option as a balanced existence was the very opposite of his goal. He did all that he could, therefore, to anchor his son firmly to the heavy, concrete world of things, deeds and experiences.

Both sides knew that – all things being equal – the law of balance would eventfully bring the Earth back onto its righteous course. It was just a question of when. For the Usurpers' part, they were banking on subverting the natural cycles long enough to allow their plan to be fully executed first. Then they would be able to spin the universal order on its axis before this balancing took place. Once this was accomplished, they would rule the universe and change the laws as they saw fit. The Celestial Fellowship, on the other hand, felt that they just had to hold things together long enough for the natural law of balance to be fully expressed. If they could just get a sufficient number of earthbound human souls to remember their true selves and radiate light throughout this dark period of planetary upheavals, then the Earth would be able to retain her identity, her people would be able to retain their souls and the Earth and the people alike would be able to move up to a higher vibratory plane of existence.

In any case, the quickening phase had begun. Richard could feel it and see it. The more intensely he felt the shift beginning, the more his decision loomed large in front of him even though he was not conscious of it yet. The Usurpers offered power as they rained death and destruction down on the world in order to create a new way of life. The Celestial Fellowship offered hope as they rained love and invitations to higher consciousness down on the world in order to create a new way of life. It all began to define itself in front of him. Out of dense fog and light mist, the two opposing forces were beginning to display themselves in plain view. For Richard and the people who inhabited Earth at this time, a choice was beginning to present itself.

24. Reaching Up

Even in their darkest hour as the great upheavals began to reshape the Earth, earthbound humans still retained the power to mitigate the effects of these catastrophes to some extent. All they had to do was reach up. However having been experimented on and tampered with for eons, the earthbound humans had become creatures who were attached to their habitual ways. They craved some sense of stability in their lives, even if it came at a high cost. They clung to the cultures, religions and societies into which they had been born life after life regardless of merit. The consumption mentality into which they had been so carefully molded had brought them down impossibly low. Reaching outside of themselves for the solutions to life's problems had made them as weak as they could possibly be. Most crippling of all, reaching out and looking down had made earthbound humans into receivers of messages and directives from the Great Usurpers and the dark planners. Most of them never questioned where they found themselves and never looked – either within or without – for something better.

But now the upheavals were obviously under way and gaining in momentum. Earthbound humans would have a way to make a leap in their development as a life form. The enormous pressure that was being applied to them by the great upheavals all over the Earth created endless opportunities – opportunities to live simply with what little was available, opportunities to look within for the solutions to life's problems, opportunities to see life for what it could be and opportunities to reach up to obtain that ideal. When earthbound humans woke up in the middle of the night feeling lost and confused in the midst of uncertainty and danger, instead of basting themselves in the gravy of their victimization, they could actually try something new. They could reach up and pray that the highest possible path to a better life would open up before themselves and their children. They could find the inner conviction to take a stand for what was highest and, on that basis, ask to be lifted up. They could find the courage and the humility to open their minds and hearts to the truths that had been waiting for them all of these centuries outside of the confines of the narrow box of their conditioning. They could determine to become the best people they could possibly be. They could offer to walk the path that would be illuminated for them if they agreed to walk it in faith and with perseverance.

Instead of asking the same old question of, "Why me?" and describing themselves in the same old way of, "Poor me," they could see the collapsing system as their opportunity to make a fresh start. They could see that there was a better way and that there always had been a better way. If even just a few of them were to open themselves up to a better way of life in a new world, then surely everything in the world could change. If even just one of them were to ascend to the highest possible level of inner development that an earthbound human being could achieve, then all of humanity could be changed forever. All they had to do was go within because by going within and reaching up, they could refashion themselves into receivers of messages and directives sent by the Celestial Fellowship. They could ask to be shown a new way, the original way, the path towards realization and galactic citizenship.

For many earthbound humans the way forward was starting to become clear. They realized that they had to reach within and reach up to connect directly to their highest Source. They had to connect and then follow the instructions that they were given in full faith that a new day was dawning and that life would be different for their brothers and sisters of the future. They had to reach up and ask for the highest path and the highest available guide or guides to lead them on that path so that they could become what they were meant to become. There is no better time than one's darkest hour to ask such questions, to pray such prayers, and to make such resolutions. Many earthbound humans did all three.

25. Becoming What We Ought to Be

It is a marked characteristic of earthbound human beings that they overwhelmingly desire pleasure, wealth, power and comforts. Yet once they start to fulfill these desires they suffer, fall, become weak of character and spirit and disconnect themselves from the God within. Hand in hand with this characteristic, the aspects of life they strive to avoid like hard work, difficult circumstances, privation, disappointments, pain, and suffering are precisely those aspects that are there to make them stronger, build better character, humble and ennoble them, and connect them to the natural world. Most importantly, learning to live harmoniously with the challenges of life opens a doorway within their hearts and allows the divine essence at the center of their beings to shine brightly and illuminate the world. In other words, their pleasures are their curse while their miseries are their blessing.

Somewhere on the very edge of his mind, just slightly out of his conscious awareness, Richard or perhaps Neil was ruminating over this state of affairs. A faint idea and remembrance of his mother's farm was lingering there in him. How hard the life there had been for him at times but for Neil that year had been a time of great growth and personal development. This was easier to see now in retrospect. The guidance embedded in this faint memory was there inside of him but it had been largely missed as the part of him that was Richard had been focused entirely outwardly occupied with watching life forms and a way of life being destroyed.

As the world collapsed thunderously around him, Richard felt swept away into weakness and helplessness just like everybody else. Even many of his powerful brethren were shocked at the grinding, hopeless poverty and overwhelming despair that had so quickly swept over the Earth. His secret guild and their dark associates had been rushed in their execution of collapsing the world economy and this had resulted in sloppy work.

The lure of extraordinary financial opportunity had made many of his brethren even greedier than they already were. They had destroyed and looted without mercy and had then pocketed much too much for themselves. The resulting chaos was worse by many orders of magnitude than what the world leaders had been told to plan for. What was happening was far beyond their ability to control or even marginally cope with. The Great War did not go as planned either. Among many other things, the nuclear missiles they had fired had had a more devastating effect on the world than originally anticipated. The powerful controllers who were tucked away in carefully chosen and constructed safe havens around the world had utterly lost control of their carefully planned out crises and collapses. Danger and despair profoundly affected even them. In fact, the entire human world was free falling at hurtling speeds. It was just at this time that the Earth herself joined in to the catastrophe by going through violent shudders and shrugs of her own. And that changed everything.

It had long been said by those with special sight that from the hearts of many human beings a desperate plea had risen up to the Creator to end the unnatural abomination that the people of Earth had inflicted upon themselves. This, they said, was in part what brought about the epic changes occurring on the Earth. It was also said by many wise ones that the Earth herself, after suffering for thousands of years the stress and destruction visited upon her by these surface dwelling parasites, had also sent a plea for help to her protector, the Sun. The Sun had heard the Earth's call and had eventually answered it by sending down a long siege of solar flares unlike any that had ever approached the Earth before. These flares sent such extraordinarily high electrical currents over the millions of miles of electrical wire now strung all over the Earth that not only were power grids knocked out and technological equipment of all kinds destroyed, but the resulting fires had incinerated large sections of the surface of the Earth. Billions of plants, animals and people were wiped out in a relatively short period of time. The electric power grids going down also caused nuclear power plants all over the world to melt down and send lethal doses of radiation spilling across the planet's atmosphere and surface and into its oceans.

As intense storms of solar flares wreaked havoc with the world, the planet's natural systems went into such a chaotic state that every remaining person on the face of the Earth knew that their world was being changed forever. The final shifting of the poles leading up to their being fully reversed began to speed up. As the magnetic field began to waver and fluctuate, a fury was unleashed that began rearranging the Earth's surface. Life on Earth became a nightmare that her inhabitants could never have imagined. Natural disaster followed upon natural disaster. The tectonic plates shifted dramatically at this time which triggered ongoing clusters of earthquakes. Volcanoes erupted. Land masses rose suddenly above the sea or disappeared equally suddenly beneath the sea. Great fires and engulfing floods came and came again. The Earth rumbled and shook and spewed and roared. The sky darkened endlessly, only cracking open periodically to emit blinding light.

Earthbound humans died by the billions as did most other forms of life. Dying was the easy path, of course. For the earthbound humans who survived, life was beyond excruciating. The intense electromagnetic activity, the vibrational condition of the Earth, the violent cataclysms that seemed never to end, and the dramatic swings in air pressure, light and temperature all drove the surviving people mad. Their nervous systems felt like they were on fire. They lived through soul killing headaches, or dropped from spontaneous heart attacks or strokes. They felt as if their bodily systems were being torn apart and that they too were being rearranged right down to the level of their DNA. People often ran wild with panic or rage or pain or grief or madness. Years went by and still the people died. Some lived, of course, but many did not.

Before the cataclysms had even started, the Great Usurpers had rendered earthbound humans too weak and too disconnected from their natural support systems for them to have the necessary strength and skill to connect with what they needed to survive this epic life-ending, world-rearranging catastrophe. Most of the people really just had no chance. Many of the Usurpers left the physical human bodies into which they had incarnated during this period of time. Instead they now attached themselves to human hosts as dark energetic entities that parasitically fed off of the despairing masses.

Most of the safe havens that the dark planners had created for themselves had been destroyed over the years. Many of the world's rulers had been killed. The ones who were left were long since running scared. With the scattering or demise of its key members, the broken down communication and travel systems, and no real ability to control the chaos, the dark planners' dream of a new world order in which they ruled over a global system was no longer possible. Worse still, the dark planners found themselves in a world of hurt personally that they had somehow not anticipated. In fact, they had been as dependent as anyone else upon the system that they had long imposed on the planet. They were helpless without their servants and their systems. They could do virtually nothing for themselves. After so many generations of wielding selfish power and feeding endless desires, they too had lost the ability to adapt and change to the new circumstances facing all of Earth's inhabitants. As a matter of fact, they had turned out to be the most helpless beings on the Earth. They had drawn all of their self-worth from exerting power and control and enjoying status and material possessions. Being focused on nothing but following the dictates of the Great Usurpers, the dark planners had put no effort into self-development over the generations. They were internally bankrupt and lost without the system that had made them important. And now that system was destroyed.

For a long while most of the members of the secret guild who had survived were still petrified. They were hiding under their rocks and praying to their Dark Overlords to spare them

176

from their inevitable comeuppance. It was only then that the few dark planners still alive finally realized that they too had been pawns all along. They were not going to get a seat at the table as there would be no table. It was plain to see now. Their dark overloads, the Great Usurpers, had played and exploited them just as the dark planners had played and exploited their own human brothers and sisters. The dark planners were slaves just like everyone else. The stinging slap of the reality of their true place in the pyramidal structure had struck them. The human vipers had served their purpose and so they were now cast aside and left to be picked apart by Nature's unforgiving hands.

This outcome had been inevitable. The laws of attraction and intention work together in creating one's life no matter whether it is a time of upheavals or not. Hostile and destructive intentions and actions eventually attract hostility and destruction to oneself in one form or another. This was common knowledge which the dark planners apparently had thought would not apply to them. Perhaps they had believed that the Great Usurpers would be able to bend the laws of the cosmos just for their sakes. But that could never be.

Evolved beings possess a powerful, godlike thought force that contains within it an unfathomable potential to create, preserve and/or destroy. When a being's thought force is used in opposition to the will of the Creator or in opposition to the best wishes of the being's own heart, an unacceptable imbalance is created within the person. Their wrongfully used thought force automatically triggers a response from Nature designed to bring the person back into balance and return the system to balance as well. The programs or chain reactions that hostile, destructive people create with their wrong thoughts are out of bounds or against the law, so to speak. Their thoughts are a perversion of the essence that suffuses the divine universe in which we all exist. As the universe works to cleanse itself of these wrongly created programs, the full brunt of the universal pushback must be expressed against the original naughty creator of the problem.

So according to inviolable cosmic law, all of the bad will, hostile intentions, greed and heartless lust for power that lay behind the destructive plans designed and executed by the secret societies of the ruling elite were eventually thrown back at them. Experiencing this pushback during the already mind-breaking time of the cataclysm completely undid them. Their collective world was shattered. So many of the so-called elite fell away that, by now, there was only a handful of stubborn dark planners left who were still looking for their chance to regain control and execute their long cherished plans.

Richard was not one of them, however. Richard never had gotten a power rush from being a part of the group that had brought the world to its knees. Long ago he had seen how shallow, delusional and narcissistic the people were who ran his order. Now after living through decades of the most intense destruction, Richard was not only devastated like everyone else but he was also devastated by the condition of soul-killing sadness and despair that pervaded the whole planet. The moaning masses' illusions and the world they had existed in had been torn apart. Everything that they had believed in was gone. So many had died already and, even now, many were giving up. They simply stopped living in one way or another. Many of the survivors wailed and cried and beseeched what seemed like a deaf God for a rescue that would never come.

This "poor me" attitude had always been the bane of the earthbound human. These poor creatures who were never given the benefit of natural evolution and who had been exploited and abused time and time again had never learned to take responsibility for their existence. As a result, they had endlessly repeated this pattern of completely wrecking themselves and their world over and over again, thus reducing themselves to a condition of begging, groveling and pleading to be saved. Over and over again they had done this. The pity was that they had so little understanding of their very own history that they didn't even know that they were repeating the same cycle time and time again.

These intelligent creatures who were known for their legendary resilience had not figured out even a few basic solutions to their unchanging problems. First of all, they never once considered that they themselves were key creators of their problems and, therefore, that they themselves were a source of their own destruction. Without recognizing this, earthbound humans could never follow this fact to its logical conclusion, i.e. if they themselves had the power and the ability to create such problems, then it stood to reason that they could also create effective solutions.

Beseeching God or some vague higher force to come rescue them was not a solution. It was only an expression of helplessness. Rather, earthbound humans had to apply the same thought force they used to create their problems towards creating solutions to their dilemmas. As the problems had existed inside of them first before they had been expressed in the physical world, solutions must have existed inside of them all of this time as well. If humans would only become conscious of this and activate their inner process for creating solutions, then solutions too could be expressed in the physical world.

In addition to realizing that solutions can be found within, there was another quite simple realization that could transform their lives and liberate earthbound humans from these destructive patterns that repeated themselves time and time again. People had not yet realized that the game they were playing – the kind of life they had been striving to live – was not natural to them. Most of them didn't even really like it. They had let a small percentage of weak and cowardly people who channeled dark forces define what human life was to be for all of them. They had allowed a cabal of dark and secretive abusers to dictate to them what success was. These deceptive, demonically possessed leaders had created a game that only they could control and only they could win and they had convinced the other 90% of humanity to play along.

The fact of the matter was that most people did not

want to be rich and powerful. They did not want the burden of excesses of stuff they didn't need and didn't use. Most people have always wanted to live day to day, allowing the natural world to provide what they needed. Most people have generally not wanted to spend their time plotting, conniving and working to secure more useless things. Instead they have wanted to spend more time being with their loved ones and creatively expressing themselves. Most earthbound humans have all along had a deep inner craving for the real goal of human life which is to become what they ought to be.

The demographics of the earthbound human personality types at the beginning of the cataclyms had been basically like this: roughly 10% were people who were spiritually evolved and capable of leading humanity in the right direction. 80% of the people were more or less passive and just did what they are told. The remaining 10% were overwhelmingly selfish, aggressive and hostile. This group lusted for power and always got it. Time and time again the third group of selfish, hostile people had tricked or lured the first and second groups of spiritual evolved people and the remaining masses into playing their game. It had rarely occurred to either the first or second group to simply say, "No thanks. We are neither going to fight you nor obey your rules. We are going to use our internal resources and power to create our own world – the world as it is meant to be." And so the aggressive 10% had ruled the day.

These two critical realizations that solutions lie within and that earthbound humans are naturally geared to live simple, intimate lives were very difficult concepts for the earthbound humans to grasp. They just had not been able to reach out and grab a hold of these positive programs and integrate them into their systems. In fact these realizations and the "programs" that supported them had been more or less invisible to humans. But Richard was beginning to sense them.

As he looked out on a world that had been reduced to an almost uninhabitable wasteland in many places, Richard slowly began to ask the right questions. He knew that his diabolical group had worked to create these problems, so why couldn't the rest of humanity work to reverse them? He also knew that humanity's evil extraterrestrial overlords had manipulated the people of Earth into going in this self-destructive direction over a long, careful orchestrated period of time. So he asked himself why the Great Usurpers hadn't just done this work themselves. Hadn't they had the power to enslave humanity outright? Had they been afraid of something?

Gradually an unshakable feeling came over Richard that he had lived through similar situations in past existences, that he had made weak choices before and had seen destruction as a result. He felt that over and over again people had suffered terribly while he had only stood by and wrung his hands at best. Richard became filled with the conviction he could not – would not – continue this pattern. He kept thinking that there must be a way out of this trap of failed past experiences. He found himself thinking about it almost obsessively. He became completely centered on his question. His inner contemplation on finding a solution to breaking this pattern deepened the craving in his heart. With his mind and heart focusing ever more completely on this one point, a powerful vacuum with tremendous pull was created in him. Richard felt strong again. He felt like he was on the cusp of something magnificent. He began reaching up and searching for a new path. He sensed that a solution was coming into view.

Richard had been a long time participant in this experiment that was finally reaching a turning point. To call earthbound humanity a controlled experiment would be ridiculous. There had been too many uncontrolled variables that had multiplied themselves over hundreds of thousands of years. There had been too many different groups of researchers, both good and evil, altering the experiment according to their own responsibilities or interests. The experiment was exceptionally far reaching as it encompassed all levels of existence from the solid material level all the way to subtle energetic bodies. No one could know for sure what the outcome of the experiment would be. The earthbound human, the subject of the experiment, was about to face its final evaluation. Would the human being reach upwards? Would it embrace its higher nature and become what it was meant to become? Or would the earthbound human become another failed attempt at genetic manipulation that would be cast atop the trash heap of other now extinct evolutionary failures?

The time of choosing was now at hand.

26. Fusion vs. Fission

Richard had finally come to the great crossroads of his life. The choice that lay before him, and his alter ego Neil, was a simple yet profound one. His choice was between following the path supported by the Celestial Fellowship or being dragged along the path marshaled by the Great Usurpers. His choice was between good and evil. His choice was between the two divergent pathways of fusion versus fission.

The path of fusion was the path provided by nature for leading a being back to its Creator. Within the scientific community and the public at large at the time, fusion was generally only recognized in the context of nuclear fusion. Nuclear fusion was the process by which a large amount of energy was added to two lighter atomic nuclei sufficient to fuse them together into a heavier nucleus. People had been interested in this process before the upheavals when sources of energy were a driving concern. Fusion had been attractive to them because it released an enormous amount of energy without any radioactive byproducts. Many earthbound humans had heard that fusion fueled the sun but that was about all that they had known. In reality, this material level of fusion was the merest reflection of the totality of fusion as an approach, of fusion as a spiritual path and as the path that nature had been and still was providing for them. The process by which particles fuse together to make a star selflessly consume itself for eons of years so that it can generously illuminate the surrounding universe only hints at the much more subtle and loving process of coming together, or fusion, that can happen in the hearts of every soul-bearing being.

The internal star that had lain dormant in the hearts of most of the soul-bearing folk across the known galaxies was the primary preoccupation of the Celestial Fellowship and the Entrusted Ones who guided them. The Celestial Fellowship's primary function was to facilitate the natural process of fusion in all and everything on all planes of existence and in every dimensional field. On earth they had particularly focused on helping earthbound humans remember that they were all connected to the Source. Members of the Celestial Fellowship relied on the fact that the call of Love is strong. When it is remembered, heard and embraced, connection to all and everything can eventually be achieved.

Earthbound humans had wrongly associated love with pleasure. Love is certainly there in pleasure as love suffuses all things but true love, Divine love, is only realized through pain. The longing pain of an awakened heart craving to merge back into the Source is what makes Divine mergence possible. Scientific fusion in the physical world on the Earth before the upheavals had required the input of tremendous heat or energy to make fusion take place. Divine fusion or fusion on the spiritual plane, however, is fueled by the intense vacuum created in a yearning heart that can no longer bear another moment of separation from its Beloved. This one-pointed, all-consuming craving to return Home brings a being to the Creator's door where the two can eventually fuse into one.

Evidence of natural or divinely directed fusion at work used to be easily found everywhere on Earth. Healthy forests had been an example. Throughout such forests, beneath the surface of the soil, the great mother trees had connected with other trees of all kinds over large distances through networks of roots and fungi and plant communities and vibrations. The trees and the plants of other kinds all around them had been similarly connected. Throughout such forests information had been passed back and forth, resources had been shared, love and support had been given. All inhabited the ecosystem together working under the guidance of Fusion to make the forest live the life that it had been meant to live.

Lucy was a being of Fusion. Her loving nature, her heartfelt sacrifice, her work of looking for and pulling out the best in people, animals, plant life, elementals and inter-dimensional beings had made her farm a mecca of Fusion. Every being that

184

had come to Lucy's farm, in whatever form it had taken and on whichever plane of existence it had lived, had connected on a heartfelt level to all and everything else that had inhabited her homestead. Love ennobles us all. Love is the subtle, irresistible force that binds us altogether and makes universal Fusion the only truth, the only reality.

This was exactly why the Great Usurpers abhorred love and never had anything to do with fusion. Instead they worshipped fission. Fission, or nuclear fission as it had been commonly called on Earth, is the unnatural and demonic process by which a large atomic nucleus is split into two or more smaller particles. This triggers a chain reaction that leads to a massive and enormously destructive nuclear explosion that also leaves behind large quantities of unnatural, dangerous, radioactive byproducts. However for the Great Usurpers, fission had always been much more than that. Fission had been a way of life that went far beyond merely scientific or even military applications.

Far, far back in history the Great Usurpers had stood at their own crossroads. Like many evolved races across the universe, they had faced a predicament that had arisen entirely out of their own freely chosen path of self-destruction. They had been on the verge of destroying their planet as well as sections of the solar system around them due to their consumerist way of life which they had magnified to overwhelming proportions through the unwise use of technology. When faced with a choice between changing their ways or ceasing to exist, their pride in their technological achievements so blinded them that they chose to create a third option. They chose to make their own way outside of the bounds of natural universal law and order.

At the moment when their world had been all but destroyed and they were cut off from their own solar body, their outer world went dark and empty. So this race buried itself in the core of their planet and used nuclear fission to power their existence. They had chosen to separate themselves from everything else in the universe in order to maintain some semblance of what they considered to be their superior way of life. They had chosen the path of fission and, consequently, had become forever more "Great Usurpers".

Fission is the complex and dangerous process of violently ripping things apart. It is a demonic process that is carried out hatefully while thumbing one's nose at the will of God. The Usurpers had derived all of their power from ripping things to pieces. The systems they created always involved tearing the very fabric of the universe apart. These were the very same systems that they had later imposed upon earthbound humans in order to quietly lead those humans away from the divinity that resided within them.

One of those systems was their long range, fission-based approach to socialization. Within the psyche of the earthbound human race existed violent tendencies and compulsions to rule over and control everything in sight. Over and over again from early history, tribes of earthbound humans had transformed themselves, largely through war, into strong and ambitious kingdoms with large armies. The kingdoms invariably had made attempts to go on expanding in order to some day rule the world. After brief periods of success in which such kingdoms had grown into even larger ruling empires, the decadent lifestyle that had always developed by this point in their development had made the people fat and lazy. The empire plateaued and then fell as it was usurped by hungrier and more aggressive groups whose empires would also later fall as apathy and compliance set into them too.

Then well over a thousand years ago now, a way to circumvent this cycle came to the minds of a group of leaders. Their empire had been in a state of decline for some time and was collapsing in the face of three hostile and ambitious tribes with varying beliefs and religions that were closing in on them from all sides. The leaders of this empire could see no way to escape and no apparent path to victory. They already knew from their own experience that conquering the world by military force was not an option and that maintaining even just a good sized empire with its necessarily enormous and expensive military force was ultimately unsustainable. There had to be another way to stay in control. There had to be a different system for retaining power and control over the world. There had to be another way to sustain and grow their empire. They searched for an answer.

The people of this empire had long practiced the dark arts and religiously carried out rituals for communicating with negative spirits. One of the problems with engaging in the dark arts is that as they are practiced in darkness, the beings the people who use the dark arts end up connecting with are duplicitous and malicious by nature. The entities with whom the leaders of this empire were primarily in contact turned out to be the Great Usurpers and the Usurpers had their own plan and agenda. So as the empire approached complete collapse in the face of the three warring tribes, the leaders and their wayward people reached out into the darkness. They groveled and sacrificed, asking for a rescue plan that would save them from their demise. In their hour of need, they bowed before their demonic gods and begged for a way out of their predicament.

Since their initial defeat on Earth so many years ago, the Usurpers had been looking for just such an opportunity as this one. They had been searching for a way to control and then subvert the world of the earthbound humans. They had waited for thousands of years for an opportunity to invisibly insert themselves into their power structure. So recognizing this situation as the perfect opportunity, the Great Usurpers gladly responded to the pleas of the ruling class of the collapsing empire. With foresight and efficiency, they uploaded their system of social power and control into the high priests of the deteriorating empire. It was a simple system of world dominance, anchored in fission, which employed such tactics as subliminal re-programming, social infiltration, and divide and conquer strategies.

By nature, earthbound humans lived best within the intimacy of family relationships. Families, in turn, cooperated together as tribes or family-based villages. Earthbound humans felt at ease in small, local groups which worked together to survive or thrive on their abundant home planet. The system the Great Usurpers ushered in, on the other hand, taught the high priests and dethroned kings henceforward how to rule their subjects through division. Their system did not show them alternate ways of building communities, armies, kingdoms or empires – not even to their own ends. Instead the newly formed dark planners were taught by the Usurpers to infiltrate already existing communities around the globe and then covertly subvert them from within and fracture them.

One iron-clad rule and one relentless two-part strategy made the system work generation after generation. The rule was one of loyalty. Always, under pain of death, must each dark planner remain loyal to the group of dark planners as a whole and its ideals. This unswerving loyalty also automatically kept each dark planner bound to his demonic overlords, the Great Usurpers. Step one of the strategy towards world dominance which fully occupied the dark planners was that of surreptitiously joining any and all earthbound human organizations, and even some families, in order to obtain power and influence behind closed doors and out of sight of any people who might catch on to their agenda. The second step, upon successful infiltration of any organization, was to divide and conquer whenever possible.

Those initial leaders of the collapsing empire who went on to become the first dark planners rapidly complied. They pledged oaths, on pain of death, to stay loyal to their secret organization. They went out into the world and joined in every organization they could. They joined religions, became citizens of countries, married into families of power and influence, and joined clubs, organizations and political parties. They learned to act like the members of the groups they infiltrated. They learned the lingo, the manner of dress and expression and lifestyle, and the views and opinions of their newfound groups. They adroitly acted just like everyone else, but at every turn and with every opportunity they steered the group towards division. Over time and with practice, the dark planners slowly extended the power of fission in the world. The empire of those first leaders was no longer a materially recognizable empire as people were used to defining empires, perhaps, but the invisible tentacles of their new-style empire of inexorable power and control would slowly consume the entire Earth.

As the years and generations passed, dark planners became persons of wealth, power and influence all over the globe. They were rarely the kings and queens of countries but rather were more craftily placed as the people who whispered in the ears of the kings and queens. Soon a world of fission began taking shape under the influence and darkly inspired actions of the dark planners who were themselves being compelled to act as puppets at the ends of the strings held in the claws of the Great Usurpers. Following instructions bit by bit over centuries, the dark planners shifted earthbound humanity from a land-based and community-based view of the world and distribution of power to a narrow focus on money power as the foundation and source of everything. With this came an ever encroaching banking system and, eventually, a debt-based monetary system that imposed massive worldwide division and separation. Each member of the new money and debt-powered society was now set up to selfishly compete with even their own family members for resources, prestige and, most of all, for an imaginary paper wealth controlled by the dark planners. This shift to money power, economic turmoil, and seeming scarcity was just one of the many wedges that the dark planners used to divide and conquer earthbound humanity.

The dark planners worked behind the scenes in every other sector of earthbound human society as well. They took positions of influence in all manner of religious and faith based organizations around the globe in order to pit religious adherents against each other. They worked within governments to pit countries and political parties against each other. Within a short period of time they perfected their divide and conquer warfare when ripping human groups apart along racial and ethnic fault lines. Dark planners joined in communities everywhere at the most local levels and from there pitted neighbor against neighbor and brother against brother. Dark controllers methodically held positions of influence from the lowest levels to the highest levels of all corners of society and on both sides of any conflict. This gave them the leverage and the organizational ability to fan the flames of hostility, pride and violence in their earthbound human brothers and sisters. Meanwhile the dark planners remained unswervingly loyal to each other and to their secret oath.

Their infiltration and subsequent control of social systems was not the only element of fission that the dark planners learned to use to build and maintain their secret empire. All of the science that the Great Usurpers gradually uploaded into successive generations of dark planners was rooted in fission as well and took fission to entirely new levels in human thought and practice. Early on, scientists were enticed into abandoning their holistic approach to studying the world around them. Instead they switched over to trying to understand what they saw through the mental and physical processes of cutting everything open and studying the dismembered parts in isolation from each other. This radical movement from wonder to doubt, from whole to part, eventually led to a global shift in human consciousness towards fission itself. Everything imaginable was fractured, dissected, analytically studied and rendered lifeless. Then the lifeless parts were put back together according to human tendencies. They were bent and twisted, if necessary, into a new whole that invariably turned out to reflect the will of the dark planners. This mental habit and practice of fission became so ingrained and so pervasive that the earthbound humans eventually mistook their fractured view of the world and themselves as actual reality.

Ultimately the dark controllers divided earthbound human beings from everything wholesome including from nature, their health and their families. Every system the earthbound humans depended upon was now based in fission. Every system the dark planners introduced to their earthbound subjects was designed to rip someone or something apart. In the crime of all crimes, all of their systems were designed to be experienced together as a dark, unnatural new way of life. They were specifically designed to sever the bond between earthbound human beings and the divinity that resided within them. After centuries of careful effort, this ultimate fission of separating earthbound humans from God was almost fully accomplished. Earthbound humans were nearly ready for the harvest.

This was the moment when Adrian came into power. He had always been expert at directing the force of fission. He had radiated fission from every pore of his body all of his life. He used to be able to just walk into a room and trigger couples in it into fighting and best friends into suddenly looking jealously at one another. His life assignment had been to be the catalyst that propelled the system into its final phase. Adrian's first task to this end had been to collapse the worldwide economic system, thereby sending earthbound humans into a state of panic driven chaos. With that accomplished, his next task had been to oversee the driving of a wedge of terror between the mass population of earthbound humans and the divinity within them.

An animal that is about to be killed by a predator is driven into a state of panic by those final moments just before being taken and eaten. It dies in a state of mindless terror. Adrian's work had been to bring all of earthbound humanity into a similar state of mindless terror. Once in this state, the humans would plead for mercy and offer anything – even their Souls – in order to not feel such soul-crushing fear any more. After extracting this level of cooperation from them, Adrian would next oversee the critical process of using nuclear fission to rip the collective Soul energy away from all of the people on Earth. From there, a few Great Usurper superiors who were thoroughly trained and anxiously waiting would harvest that Soul energy and harness it to immediately split the fabric of the universe into bits and pieces. In the aftermath, the Great Usurpers would remake the universe in their own image with themselves as the new god. This new universe would be an abomination. It would be a divided universe in which every particle worked selfishly and hostilely to fulfill its own desires at the expense of everything else.

Without knowing it, Richard was now at the center of this battle between fusion and fission. He had been groomed by his earthly father to be a dark angel of division. He had long since seen all that was wrong with his earthly brothers and sisters and had lost hope for them or even interest in them. He had been completely encased in heavy materialism. His inner connection to the divinity within him had been all but forgotten. On the surface, Richard was seemingly the product of a system of fission. He had turned away from the sun. He was unable to feel the Divine Father within him.

But on a deeper level Richard was awakening to a call from the innermost depths of his heart. He had long been asking more and deeper questions. He had long been slowly waking up to the atrocities of the status quo and the fraudulent nature of the ruling class. Now that their plans and actions for collapsing the entire planetary system had manifested so violently, there was no denying who the dark planners were and the fact that they were evil. The story had all but reached its conclusion. Despite any rationalizations or excuses, the dark controllers were obviously the villains in this epic.

Knowing all that he knew and having experiencing all that he had experienced, Richard could see only darkness all around him. However, his mother's love still flickered within him. It nurtured the bond between Neil and his Divine Father. Somehow there was a faint whisper all about now, one that Richard could not clearly hear but could feel deep within him. His Divine Father, the Master of Fusion, was calling to him. He was saying, "Remember, my son, and come home."

27. Adrian's Pitch

By the time both sides of the extraterrestrials allowed themselves to be openly seen by the earthbound humans, the Earth itself was in pretty bad shape. Most of the people who were still alive after the upheavals led impoverished, broken down lives of scrounging and scavenging. The more highly spiritually developed humans, having been somewhat shielded from the full brunt of the destruction, were working towards salvaging something for the future of humanity both in terms of the Earth itself as well as any possibilities for social and spiritual progress for earthbound humans.

The few remaining living members of the secret ruling class were grasping helplessly at anything they could to regain their lost position as world rulers. They interpreted the return of the extraterrestrial races to Earth as an opening to rally humanity together to fight a common invading enemy with themselves at the helm. They had actually set the stage for exactly such a scenario before the upheavals had started by implanting ideas about such an occurrence throughout the media. Furthermore, both then and now they were able to tap into an archetype buried deep within the human psyche, as there was an historical human reference point, a shared ancestral memory of earthbound humans from the distant past having joined together to fight off the Great Usurpers once before. However, this last futile attempt by the dark planners to regain control was nothing more than a Hail Mary pass thrown into a hurricane. Their plans had come to fruition, after all. It was just that the fruit of those plans was the total destruction of the system they once thought they dominated.

Meanwhile Adrian was now advanced in age and had developed terminal cancer. His time on Earth was almost up. In past years he had been in his glory as he had worked to take down humanity and his work had gone extremely well. With each successful completion of a phase of his plan, Adrian found that he regained a little more consciousness about his real origin and increased his awareness about the true nature of the demons he prayed to. Gradually he had been remembering his real life as a Great Usurper. As Adrian's earthly life was coming to a conclusion, he no longer considered himself a human. In fact, he was eagerly awaiting his reward after this life ended. After all, his work had been impeccable. He would surely re-emerge as a powerful ruler within the Great Usurper hierarchy.

Adrian had one final, critical piece of work to do, however. He had to convince his son to bring his own life's work to its apotheosis by carrying out the final stages of the Great Usurpers' grand assignment. Having Richard carry on his work had always been Adrian's plan and his goal. But now Richard's continuation of the work was essential because the uncontrolled damage to the planet and the unanticipated demise of much of the secret guild's structure and membership left no one else to hold the plan together. Richard's role in the Great Usurpers' plan was now mandatory. Adrian knew that there was a great opportunity for Richard in that and that it was now his job to persuade, or manipulate if need be, his son into fulfilling the glorious destiny that awaited him.

Years ago after putting considerable effort into Richard's training, Adrian had more or less given up on him. He had sensed a lingering and alien softness in Richard that he knew would only be a dangerous weakness in the end. As traces of this softness persisted even in the face of Adrian's forceful efforts to stamp it out, Adrian eventually deduced that his son would probably be unsuitable for filling his shoes. He had turned his attention away from Richard from then on. Besides, when his own efforts had been so successful and the onset of the great upheavals had been triggered at long last, Adrian figured that the plan had been executed sufficiently that Richard would not be necessary for its completion anyway. However now that the situation had gone terribly awry, Adrian was in the uncomfortable position of needing Richard. Clearly Adrian's assignment could

194

no longer be considered successfully completed without Richard stepping into his shoes.

For his part, Richard had a growing distaste for his father and his father's blood lust. He saw a deep malevolence in his father that far exceeded anything that had existed in the other members of the secret guild, many of whom were pretty sadistic in their own right. Many times when he was younger, Richard had observed his father experiencing pure joy while engaged in his work of utterly degrading the people of Earth. It was creepy to the point of being otherworldly in some unnamable way.

Back in the day, the other dark planners had been sadists who relished the rush of power they felt from inflicting suffering on others. Richard himself had experienced this rush of power that came from being in control of the fate of so many. Power and control can be quite intoxicating. There was a big difference, though. Richard noticed that when his brethren went into an abusive mode, they literally entered an altered state of consciousness. Their eyes changed and what was behind their eyes changed as well. It was as if they were possessed by demons.

Richard had observed over the years that this was not the case with his father. His father did not lose consciousness or seem possessed as he ordered the destruction and suffering of so many. On the contrary, his father seemed to become more of who he really was. He was congruent when he inflicted pain on the people of Earth. For Adrian, it was similar to someone experiencing pure ecstasy from exterminating cockroaches in their infested house. It was as if Adrian had battled these human cockroaches for thousands of years and, after careful planning, he was finally getting his victory over them.

As Richard had gained some independence and distance from his father, he had grown more reflective and had begun seeing his father for who he really was. For the last some years he had been totally repulsed by his father's malevolent and sadistic nature and intended never to see him again. In fact, it had been about five years since they had seen each other. They had

had a falling out then which had really been a superficial expression of the growing tension between them. At that point Adrian had forgotten about his son and Richard had moved on from his father. Since Adrian no longer showed any interest in him and Richard himself wanted no part of his father, Richard believed that their relationship had ended. That was until the day Adrian tracked down his son and made his pitch for Richard to follow in his father's footsteps and take over where he was leaving off.

Adrian had never really talked with his son as he had put all of his focus over their years together into shaping him. As a result they had no real relationship but rather merely a heavy and undeniable connection. Even at this important juncture, Adrian did not set out to win Richard's heart over to his view as winning hearts was just not what he did. Rather he treated Richard in the same way that he treated everyone else, only more so. So Adrian's strategy with his son was to take everything away from him that was human, thus leaving him with only one choice. That one choice would be for Richard to carry out the final actions required by the Great Usurpers so that they could harvest the collective Soul energy of earthbound humanity.

Now, at the end of his life, Adrian realized that his soul was not of the human variety so he technically could not make the choice for humans to give up their souls. No, this momentous choice had to come from a human, a past leader of men who had the stature to lead his fellow earthbound slaves into giving up what was most precious to them. Adrian finally understood the need for a son and, therefore, the utility of his union with Lucy. It would take a genuine human to throw the switch and turn off the light within earthbound humanity forever.

After something of a search, Adrian located where Richard was hidden away from the apocalyptic forces that ravaged the earth and promptly made his way to the spot without giving any forewarning to Richard. Richard was shocked to see his father suddenly show up on his doorstep one afternoon. His shock was not only because his appearance was unexpected but because

196

Adrian was not someone who went to people. People went to him. Before even crossing the threshold, Adrian could see that Richard wanted no part of him and was not about to willingly consent to carrying out the work he had for him. This was of no consequence and did not affect Adrian one way or the other.

The secret societies that had executed the Great Usurpers' plans had developed tremendous technologies over the years for forcing people to do their bidding. They had installed leverage points within each human system which they could access at will to control human behavior and they had employed all sorts of broad based societal strategies for molding earthbound humans into obeying their will. They had carefully trained and educated humanity in a way that would ultimately lead them into the full cooperation the dark planners sought. On top of all of this, humans were perennially lost and looking for someone outside of themselves to rescue them. Their dark rulers knew this and had become expert at playing the part of rescuer.

Having always had all of these advantages to work with, Adrian habitually spoke to earthbound humans as if the fulfilling of his desires was inevitable and any thought in them of resisting his will was impossible. He spoke with complete authority out of his conviction that what he was saying was the ultimate truth. This was the place from which Adrian spoke even now while making his pitch to his son. He spoke to Richard as if Richard had no choice. Adrian was simply outlining Richard's destiny to him which was to do Adrian's bidding.

This was to be a battle, however. The battle began with Adrian announcing to Richard that it was now time for him to fulfill the role he was born to execute. Richard scoffed at this. He said that he wanted no part of the evil that Adrian and his secret society had visited on the planet and were surely plotting to continue visiting on the planet. Richard went on to also blame Adrian personally for some of the more egregious acts of abuse that had been carried out. He let loose and talked about how the dark planners had placed cruel and sadistic people –

many of them rapists and pedophiles – into law enforcement positions around the globe so that they would wreak havoc and inflict great tortuous pain on innocent people everywhere. He talked about the cannibalism and large execution camps that had sprung up, all of which could be traced directly back to Adrian. Yes, he saw his father's handy work everywhere he looked. Richard spoke heatedly of the many, many atrocities which he had either witnessed himself or had researched in some depth which could all be linked in some way to his father.

Richard's father did not deny or defend any of his actions. He did not show the slightest bit of defensiveness, remorse or regret about any of Richard's accusations. In a matter of fact tone, he simply replied to his son that there were no innocent people. Then he moved on to the heart of his pitch. "Richard," he said, "humanity is a failed experiment and humans are the scourge of the universe. They are an abomination." Adrian expanded on this by saying that after many interventions by a large array of extraterrestrial beings over thousands of years, humanity had still failed to evolve. The species could only be considered genetically flawed and both incapable and unworthy of being a civilized member of the universe.

Adrian paused for a time as he read his son. He could see that Richard was somewhat swayed by his argument. Richard had seen the dark things people were capable of doing. He had experienced humanity's inability to live peacefully together. He had witnessed their willful destruction of their natural world. He had seen how their aggression, greed and gluttony had dominated them. He had seen how people had rationalized their dark attitudes and excused their behaviors. He had struggled with how easily people believed in lies and myths and rejected truth over and over again. He was aware that he himself had participated in much of what was wrong with the people of Earth. He knew that there had been countless times in which he himself had demonstrated the very weaknesses that plagued his people. Under the agonizing weight of these thoughts and realizations,

Richard searched his mind for something hopeful. He tried to recall something good that existed in his world. He tried but he could not come up with anything.

Watching all of this play over Richard's face, Adrian then told him what had to be done. Humanity was a parasite that needed to be exterminated before it spread across the universe. Adrian went on to explain to Richard that there was a great society comprised of many types of extraterrestrial beings that formed a ruling council. He said that the council had ruled that humanity must be eradicated. He told him that once the people of Earth had been annihilated, their soul energy could be harvested, cleaned and put back into the universal system. Adrian told Richard in a collegial tone that they had both been sent down to complete this important task of annihilation. He said that he knew that he was dying so the rest of the work must necessarily fall on Richard's shoulders to complete. Richard had been born to this and had been trained for it. He was ready. Adrian assured him that once he completed this task, he would be elevated to a high position in another world as a different and more evolved life form. He would be rewarded for completing his father's work even as he, Adrian, was soon going to go on to his reward.

Adrian sat back and looked at his son. He had him. Richard was silent but Adrian could see it and Richard knew that he could. The deal had been closed. Adrian had successfully gotten his son to forget his own true nature and the true nature of humanity. Richard would do his bidding and the mission would be a success. Adrian then talked deep into the night and very carefully went over each step of the plan and what Richard would need to do complete it. He discussed every contingency and every possible obstacle. Adrian left nothing to chance. He filled Richard with the power he needed to complete these tasks. Finally, he sat back and looked proudly at his son.

Adrian relaxed for the first time in his life. His work would be a success. His mission was over. He had successfully carried out his orders and was now free to escape this life as a human. Adrian was very, very pleased. Within three days, he would be dead and his soul would be making its way back to his rightful place with his fellow Great Usurpers. But for now, this was his moment of Earthly glory. He had won the game and was basking in the glow of his success. It was then that Adrian had a very faint human reaction. Ever so slightly, he experienced the kind of warm, glowing feeling people have when they have just completed a life goal.

Perhaps it was being in a human body that betrayed Adrian at the most important moment of his life. Perhaps a benevolent being who was monitoring the situation gave him the idea. Perhaps it was just scripted that way. It does not matter. What matters is that as Adrian gazed at his son in his moment of triumph, he had a very self-destructive thought. He caught it as soon as it entered his mind and pushed it away but still the thought got past him and made a landing. The light and inno-cent thought was that something about Richard reminded him of his wife, Lucy.

As soon as Adrian realized that he was comparing Rich-ard to Richard's mother, he quickly forced the thought out of his mind. Then he realized that his thought represented the one flaw in his plan. For Richard to be successful in carrying out his assignment, he had to forget everything about his mother and repudiate everything of his mother that may still lurk within him. If Richard remembered any part of the true inner nature of humanity, his will would falter and his work would fail.

Adrian quickly snapped himself back from the human emotion that had briefly touched him. Still slightly rattled by the thought of his wife and the human emotions that had opened the door to such a thought, he did not notice that something had changed in Richard. His son had picked up on his thought and had begun thinking about his mother himself. Unable to do anything more, Adrian said his goodbyes to his son. With his life energy fading away, he went back to his solitary mansion to

200

await his release from the Earthly prison he had been sentenced to for so many years.

Soon after his father left, the spell that he had woven around Richard began to unravel. "My mother," Richard thought. "Yes, of course, my mother." He suddenly felt his mother's presence all around him. The thought flashed through his mind that his father's web of lies did not describe his experiences with his mother. With a rush of memories, he remembered their time together when he was a child. He remembered his visits to her farm and thought about the people who had surrounded her. How could he have so easily forgotten? These people were certainly not a form of parasite that must be eradicated. Well, there must be hope. There must be another way. At that moment, something caught Richard's eye. Lying on the floor just inside his front door, he discovered what looked like a tattered and well worn envelope.

The postal service, mail carriers and other delivery services had disappeared long ago. Travel was almost impossible and very dangerous. Fuel was hard to come by and the roads and other infrastructure had been more or less obliterated. And yet, somehow, an envelope had been slid under Richards's door. Richard was stunned as he gazed at it. With a bit of lovely handwriting on the front and the inviting glow of thick well-made paper, it lay there as a subtle reminder of a past civilization that no longer existed. Richard picked it up and gazed at it. He felt the weight of it in his hand. He turned it over and back again. There was no address or return address on it. Rather, there was a simple statement written on it in a familiar hand which said:

"To my dearest Neil ~"

28. Lucy's Letter

Once the great upheavals had begun to overwhelm the Earth, all of the creatures that inhabited the planet suffered in one way or another. No area of the planet was left unaffected. No life form was left untouched. All species suffered and the earthbound humans suffered most of all. The innocent suffered along with the guilty. However because of the law of attraction, the people who had been living more refined lives at a higher vibrational frequency did not sustain as much damage as might otherwise be expected. They did not attract direct hits, so to speak, the way the vast majority of people did and so they were personally spared to a large degree from the full impact of the planetary corrective actions.

Besides there was also the matter of some groups of earthbound humans being needed in the future for repopulating the Earth and remaking humanity. In the perfect system that is the universe, beings with desirable qualities that are willing to sacrifice and serve for the common good are often kept around. Those that are hell-bent on self-destruction are made extinct in due course. Beings with genetic attributes that are in harmony with the subtle vibrational condition at the base of all creation thrive eventually. As it turns out, the dark ones who had been practicing the dark arts had essentially targeted themselves for extinction during this great cleaning period. Those who were willing to serve out of love for the Creator, on the other hand, were rewarded with the work of rebuilding humanity and reset-tling the planet. They were also gifted with the responsibility and work of cleaning up the earth-wide mess. Furthermore, if they were able to rise above the fear, the chaos and the suffer-ing that now engulfed the world and go inside themselves, they would be able to clearly see that the world was changing for the better. With each catastrophic event, another layer of collective spiritual grossness was peeled off of the Earth. The condition on the planet was becoming lighter and lighter and this gave energy and hope to the people who had future-oriented work to do.

Small groups of people all around the planet were learning to follow their inner guidance and begin preparing themselves and their children for the upcoming paradigm shift. They built small havens where people could live together and once again connect with the natural world, grow their own food and make the shift from obsessive materialism to a life of rhythm and intuition and relationship. These pockets of the future became the small pebbles that landed in the center of the pond and sent gentle ripples of change outward toward humanity and the Earth at large.

Lucy's farm had always been such a place. Lucy had created a simple and natural movement within herself and that condition had naturally radiated out from her and touched many other people. Her farm had been a lighthouse for her village which, in turn, had become a light for all of humanity. Under her loving influence, one heart at time had long ago started to embrace the good old ways. Everyone who had lived within a 25 mile radius of her farm had been consciously affected while many other loving Souls scattered all over the Earth had also been affected on more subtle planes of existence.

By the time the great upheavals had begun to create chaos on the planet and in the lives, minds and hearts of its earthbound humans, the people of Lucy's village were largely prepared. Since they had already long since started to internalize their existence, they were accustomed to receiving warnings and instructions in their dreams and meditations and they had the skills and support to act on those warnings and instructions effectively. As a result, they had long since started adjusting themselves to the way the world was going to be instead of basing their futures on a dying system. They had also trained and prepared their children for the harsh conditions that would inevitably befall them in the future. The whole community of people had worked on their inner character and had strived to make something of themselves. They had had a change of heart and, as a consequence, had had a change of life and a change of future.

The changes that they had experienced in their hearts had purified their thoughts and changed the energetic condition in the atmosphere around them. The whole village and the people who inhabited it had become more and more refined as did the vibrational condition that they emitted. The condition of the community had become light and subtle. So when the catastrophes came looking for places to take root, they could not gain a foothold in Lucy's village.

This process worked in two ways. First, people with pure hearts and spiritual capital were automatically drawn to safe, subtle places that were not likely to see massively destabilizing events. Secondly, by working on themselves and getting closer to the divinity that was within them, these people had made themselves valuable to the Creator and invaluable for the evolutionary process. They had also drawn the attention of the Celestial Fellowship who had used their highly developed thought force to put a spiritual bubble of protection around the place. Then as the villagers' positive work created an increasingly subtle and divine condition, ever more highly developed souls were drawn to the place as were special children who were looking for a proper environment in which to incarnate. Lucy was a master gardener and her garden became a garden of hearts that bloomed and shone enough to become one of the beacons of light for all of humanity.

Lucy herself did not fare as well, though. It is true that she lived in a protected place and was spared the brunt of the brute force that ripped up the Earth. However like all highly evolved souls, Lucy was extremely sensitive. Her soft heart was open to the world so she felt the pain and misery that her fellow beings were experiencing. In many ways she felt their pain on a deeper level than they themselves felt it. And like all great souls, she took much of their pain upon herself.

As the upheavals continued, Lucy's physical condition

worsened. She often felt like she could no longer bear the suffering. She found herself praying to be liberated from her life on Earth so that she could return to her celestial home. However, that was not to be as her work was not yet finished. During the last few years of the upheavals, Lucy became so weak that she had trouble making contact with the divine spirits that supported her. This added immeasurably to her suffering. In moments of emotional weakness, she worried that her Divine Father had left her. She began thinking that she was a failure. She was convinced that she would never again see her beloved son, Neil, and that he had been lost to the dark side. During her last days before her grand ascension, her heart was filled with complete despair.

The truth was that her Divine Father was with her more than ever and surrounding her with his all encompassing love. In fact, there were many great souls constantly around her. They were all waiting for the right time for Lucy to complete her work and be released to the Divine abode that awaited her.

When that time came, Lucy was just days away from being guided back to her real home. Her human body was worn out and she had almost nothing left. The great Souls that were around her and in her heart were preparing to escort her to the Celestial Heaven. But first she had one more task to complete. She gathered up every ounce of energy that she had left and poured it into a letter to her son. It was no ordinary letter. As she wrote it, Lucy also transmitted her essence directly into her son. The letter was surrounded with refined consciousness and infused with Divine Love. The perfectly timed letter found Neil at the exact right moment. It was so arranged that when he read it in a receptive state, all of the love that she had in her enormous heart would pour into his heart. Within moments of receiving it, her Neil opened up the letter and quickly read it.

My Dear Heroic Son,

It is now time for you to become what you are meant to become. From the very moment that your loving heart began beating inside me so many years ago, you were locked in the middle of an epic battle between two vast, opposing forces. One side was represented by your father while the other side was represented by me. Our battleground was your tender young heart. While one side was attacking your heart until it became as hard as stone so that you would lose your ability to connect with your Self within, the other was nurturing your heart with pure love in order to expand it so that one day your heart would encompass the whole universe.

It was a terrible burden to put on a little boy. Many were the times that I wept myself to sleep over it. Always I prayed for a way that I could spare you from this painful war. However as my Divine Father reminded me time and time again, your Soul volunteered for this assignment. Indeed, you came with all of the inner strength you needed to not only bear the pain but to emerge triumphantly in the end. The inner conflict that has dominated your existence thus far is coming to an end now, my son. It is time for you to choose sides, one way or the other, and fulfill your destiny as a leader for your chosen side.

I believe as you read this letter that your father will have already made his proposal to you about how he expects you to proceed with your life and his work. Perhaps under the accumulated weight of the dark things and places you have experienced in this troubled world, your father has succeeded in getting you to forget your Universal Nature. If so, this would be very understandable. It would appear logical to anyone who has seen the evil that the people of Earth have brought upon themselves that the only way to stop that growing evil is to destroy the human race. There is another more hopeful option, however.

It is true that humanity is in a dark place. This is due in part to humanity's collective choices and the plans and actions of

206

*their leaders over so many years. In fairness, though, it is also due
to the many unwelcome interventions by beings from other planets
who have their own agenda for the Earth and for humans. While
it is hard to see past the greed, hostility and selfishness that humans
have indulged in for so long which has led them to the brink of destroying their world and themselves, humans do have another side.
They have a side which both you and I have experienced.*

*In this life of mine, I have experienced a great deal of hu-
man love. As a mother the love I have in my heart for you, my dear
son, has no limits. It will go on forever and it will be there long
after I shed my failing body. It is the purest love. The same love
created the universe and characterizes the Divine Being people of
the Earth call God. God is in the human heart. So in spite of all of
the dark thoughts, words and deeds that humanity has expressed,
they also have in their hearts the same Divine essence that created
the universe. I have experienced this in my human heart and, my
beloved son, I have also seen this Divine love in your heart as well.*

*Those first years of your life that we spent together remain
the happiest days I have spent on this desperate planet. I saw your
pure essence and enjoyed it more than I can say. You are a strong,
kind being who is capable of wise and effective leadership. You
have a very loving heart. Your ability to endure the pain of love is
extraordinary and most unusual in the human condition. Many
humans strive to love but the pain that goes with loving is often
too much for them to bear so they go numb and forget instead. You,
my gallant son, can bear this pain of love as well as the general
pain of others. You can bear all of the pain while staying true to
your inner calling of leading the people of Earth to a new plateau
of human achievement. This is a gift.*

*As your loving mother, it is hard for me to see anything
other than your pure and noble nature. However, it is perhaps
also a quality of yours to get lost. There may be a tendency in you
to become overwhelmed and so succumb to the many dark tempta-*

tions that have been woven around humans for destructive reasons. Once the connection to the soul is lost, it is easy for a person to forget their true purpose. A lost person becomes cynical and hard of heart, often mocking the simple and natural ways that nurture the human spirit from within. This modern system which has been planned in secret for thousands of years has now finally achieved its goal of bringing the people of Earth to their knees.

In the midst of this devastating emptiness that has swept over the Earth, there is room now for a new system based on merging "the old ways" with new harmonious and natural technologies. It is right there to be had by the earthbound humans, if they would only choose to embrace it. You, my son, are capable of leading your earthbound brothers and sisters on a path that will surely bring about exactly this beautiful change. Your work is simple. You have to remember. You have to remember the love in your heart and connect to and become the Divine Being that is your true Self. From there your heart will guide you.

Do you remember your time here on our farm when you were in high school and how you were eventually able to just know what to do and how to do it? This is your family farm now. From this very garden where I sit writing to you, you may begin your quest of helping humanity with remembering their inner nobility. With every heart-led step you take, you will find whatever inner guidance and support you need for completing your mission. The people and the resources will be provided to you even when all hope appears to be lost. There will be divine beings and ancient extraterrestrial souls monitoring your every step. They will provide loving suggestions at your request and surround you with their love. And I will not leave your side until the glorious day that you and I are reunited in a place far less harsh than our current residence.

I cannot fully express my love for you with this limited form of communication. We certainly have come to a very dense world for our life together as mother and son. The immense strug-

gles that earthbound beings go through seem too harsh to me and I wish that it all could be lighter. I wish for the Earth and her inhabitants that they be a pure reflection of the divine Creator. However, the world as it is now is what humans have made it. Only we humans can recreate the world into what it should be. I know that the challenges before you are great. Many gallant souls have walked away in defeat when faced with the burdens you are now about to bear.

However, my dear son, the upliftment of humanity is such a noble and worthwhile work. You are truly blessed to have been given this assignment. I have gazed into your loving heart all of your life and I have always seen such a wonderful and capable being in you that it fills my heart with joy to have had the honor of having been your mother. You may doubt yourself but in my heart there is no question that you will remember and that through remembering, you will be triumphant.

With all of my love and blessings,
Maaji

29. The Choice

Neil put down the letter. Tears were streaming down his face. He was filled with so many conflicting emotions that a lesser being would have been driven to complete breakdown. He closed his eyes and attempted to find the love in his heart that his mother had written of so convincingly. He was too restless, though, and filled with so many thoughts that he could not feel any one thing no matter how much he tried. He was so agitated by the effort that he wanted to pull his hair out and scream.

For three days it went on like this. He paced around the rooms of his house madly talking to himself, and making involuntary movements and gestures as he acted out past memories and experiences as they came up. He was filled with feelings of shame and despair as he remembered wretched things that he had done and crimes that he had committed against nature. Whenever he closed his eyes, his mind filled with horrific images of the hell that humans had created on their very own prison planet.

He felt all of it. He heard all of it. He saw all of it. He tasted all of it. He became all of it. He became the pain – an awful soul killing pain of a species having its essence literally torn away from it. He heard the inner screams rising up out of the hearts of the masses of earthbound humans as dark forces tugged away, loosening up the precious light that was in their hearts. Richard was being driven to madness. He could not bear the insane pain. A skin crawling restlessness made him want to jump off a cliff. For the first time, he wanted to physically hurt himself so that some kind of outer pain could overshadow the maddening pain he felt raging and roiling inside. He banged his head against a wall. He banged it and banged it until he mercifully lost consciousness for a brief while.

Richard came to, feeling even worse. His head was now throbbing sickly even as the inner darkness continued to consume him. The soul stealing instructions his father had given him flitted through his mind. It occurred to him that probably the only way to stop this unbearable pain was to complete the final step of his father's diabolical plan. He should just go ahead and finish tearing the souls away from humanity in one quick step. Their souls were dangling before him like a child's baby tooth hanging by a thread. If he just gave them a yank, surely the pain would stop and he could put a final end to this earthly madness.

He envisioned this briefly and imagined the sweet relief that would follow. He thought about it for a moment more. Involuntarily Richard shuddered. No, he could not go through with it. He could not obey his father's orders knowing as he did that humanity still had a chance to redeem itself. He reached for his mother's letter again, settled himself in a chair and read it through once more very slowly and carefully. This time he felt her words being transmitted directly into his heart. By the time Richard had finished reading it, he was calm enough to gently close his eyes and turn his attention towards his inner universe. For some time, his mind was full of thoughts but they soon faded away like the sound of a barking dog that eventually blends into all of the other sounds of the night. His restlessness began to fade as well. His consciousness drifted slowly to the center of his heart.

And then it hit him. A force that felt infinitely more powerful than he was gently entered into him but was nevertheless so strong that it pushed him hard against the back of his chair. After a moment or two, Neil realized that he wasn't breathing but that something was breathing for him. Every muscle in his body began to tense. Every cell in his body contracted. He began to shake. He thought he was going to cry out at the top of his lungs but the muscles in his neck and jaw were so tight that he could neither open his mouth nor operate his vocal chords. Fear swelled up inside him. The fear was then followed by an experience of every other possible human emotion parading through his system, one at a time, in an uncomfortable

211

and sometimes painful procession.

Once the parade of emotions ceased and the experience faded from his system a little bit, Neil found that he was filled with a deep sadness. He felt that he was going to weep as he had never wept before. Before he could shed a single tear, however, his body convulsed for a moment. His face suddenly filled with a big smile as his chest was pulled upward until it pointed at the heavens. Something heavy was quickly pulled from his heart. The four evil entities that had surrounded him and fed off him since his early contact with the secret guild years and years ago were forced out of Neil's system as they could not bear the illuminated brilliance that now emanated from his spiritually awakened heart. Demonic spirits that they were, the entities fled into the darkness screaming shrilly as they went. As soon they left him, Neil's muscles tightened even more as something very dense was wrenched from his heart. Neil fought with himself to remain calm and to continue breathing as normally as he could. Finally just when he felt that he could no longer stand the excruciating tension, one last tug yanked the gross spiritual matter from his heart. He could sense it leave as he collapsed into his seat. Then his body relaxed as if experiencing relaxation for the first time ever in his life. Minutes passed and then, ever so faintly, he heard himself say the word, "Yes."

As Neil opened his eyes and his consciousness returned to the room, he laughed from the deepest part of his heart. It was no ordinary laugh. It was a pure, quiet laugh that emanated from the core of his being. It was as if Neil had just heard the greatest inside joke ever told which made him laugh with delight. As the joke was too refined for words, Neil experienced it as a feeling at the center of his being. A crude translation of it into concepts could go something like this: the straight line of the joke would be all of the complex, heavy, mindboggling, sophisticated, burdensome and needless pursuits ever devised by the human race. The punch line of the joke would be the greatest, lightest feeling that Neil had ever experienced in his

212

life. It was the faintest, merest suggestion of a condition that all earthbound humans were born with. It was a reflection of the real goal of their lives and was to be found in their hearts. It was infinitely lighter than a feather, softer than a cloud and fainter than a whisper but it had the power of the creation of the entire universe behind it. And all you had to do at any point to find it was look inside.

There it was. At long last, Neil had remembered the love that was inside of him. He had rediscovered his true purpose. He was filled with such hope and joy now. He wanted to go to the tallest mountain top and shout to the world, "All of the silly pursuits that have created so much unnecessary suffering are just an illusion. The true gift and purpose for your lives has been right there in your hearts all along."

Neil felt reborn. He went outside. As he gazed at what was left of the world around him, he felt as if he were seeing it for the first time. The polluted air smelled better. The scorched trees looked beautiful. The faint glow of the sun behind the smoke and ash was inspiring. The world such as it was could still be beautiful. It was true that it was nearly destroyed and, in truth, the Earth and the humanity that inhabited it had fallen into a deep abyss. Neil realized that he was starting at rock bottom. "But," he thought to himself optimistically, "from this starting point of complete despair we will begin our journey upward."

Neil thought about his mother again. It flashed into his mind that he needed to see her once more. He focused his will on making a mad dash. He threw together a few things and left his house without a plan, without transportation and without even a complete understanding of the exact location of his mother's farm. Given the total collapse of the world's infrastructure, he had no idea how to get to her even if he had known exactly where she was. However, that did not matter and he knew it.

As it turned out, every step of the way Neil just knew what to do. He found people to help and guide him. He found ways of getting around and he even found ways of avoiding the marauding, murderous hoards that patrolled the roads looking for food and slaves. His newfound inner guidance helped him pick out such a good path that even the packs of wild dogs were unable to detect his scent.

Whenever he felt lost, he simply paused, concentrated on the problem for a few minutes and then followed the faint and yet potent feeling in his heart that guided him unerringly to his next step. During the times when there was no clear direction, he waited until one emerged. Finally after a seemingly impossible trip, Neil arrived at his mother's farm. Only slightly noticing the palpable change in atmosphere as he crossed into Mountain & Stars Farm, Neil rushed to his mother's earthship and walked into the front room which was filled with her many local supporters. He greeted them gently as they were all in tears. Lucy's loved ones, the villagers, were sitting silently outside of her bedroom in vigil. One of the older farmhands recognized Neil and directed him to go inside and see his mother. Once he entered the room, he found her lying in bed dying.

To most people, it would have appeared that his mother was all alone in her room. Now, however, Neil could see again so he was able to perceive many magnificent beings of pure spirit hovering around her. There was one simple and humble being in particular who looked like an old grandfatherly man of humble means. As Neil gazed at him, though, he saw that the heart of this humble being contained the whole universe. The ageless spirit turned and gazed lovingly into his eyes. Time stopped and Neil felt completely enveloped in a sense of wellbeing as he gazed back. After a few moments, Neil remembered his purpose for being there and tore his eyes away to quickly turn his attention back to his mother.

Lucy looked up at her son. She had held on to life for what seemed like weeks, hoping against hope that he would read her letter and come to her. Now that he was finally there and she could drink in his face and heart, she began to slip away from the world. Just before all of the elevated souls surrounding her prepared to escort her back to her original home, Neil reached out and took her hand. He looked deeply into her moist eyes and said, "Maaji, I remember."

The Art of Remembrance Trilogy

The Art of Remembrance Trilogy is an interdimensionally inspired series written to encourage intrepid souls as they navigate the unprecedented transformation taking place within the modern day human being. The fascinating narrative spanning hundreds of years takes the reader through this sweeping transformational process. Along the way, it also describes the magnificence of the Entrusted Ones as well as exposes the skulduggery of the demonic Appropriators. *The Choice* leads the reader from collapsing modern civilization to the dawn of a new spiritual era. *Egregore* continues in a bleak post-apocalyptic world in which life is harsh but spiritual transformation is glorious. *Galactic Citizenship* concludes with genetically and spiritually uplifted human beings living on an ennobled Earth who have graduated from the third dimensional slave status that has long held sway on our planet to multidimensional beings who have access to universal resources.

The Art of Remembrance Trilogy is a mind-blowing read, epic in scope, that not only finally makes sense of today's world but also has tools and critical perspective embedded within it that will help readers step into the new world that is slowly taking shape. The author experienced these books as channeled information coming through him that utilized well his many years of dedicated research, experience and meditative practice.

About the Author

Paul Romano lives with his wife and children in the beautiful mountains where they practice being ethyrical farmers, alternative builders, ardent homeschoolers, practitioners of the old ways, and spiritual researchers. Mr. Romano's inspiration for his work comes from his twenty year association with the Shri Ram Chandra Mission.

Please visit Paul and Leslie Romano at Bamboo Grove Press to see more titles of books and ebooks on spirituality, simple living and children written to help you persevere through the great change. http://www.bamboogrovepress.com

To learn more about the Romano family's homesteading and homeschooling adventures, please visit them at their Pockets of the Future web site at http://pocketsofthefuture.com/

Made in the USA
Middletown, DE
20 November 2015